RUNNING
SCARED

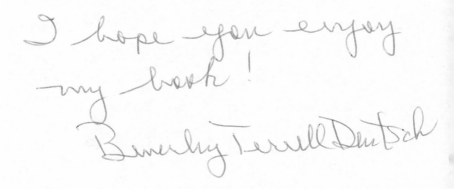

I hope you enjoy
my book!

Beverly Terrell Deutsch

RUNNING
SCARED

BEVERLEY TERRELL-DEUTSCH

Red Deer Press

Published in Canada by Red Deer Press
195 Allstate Parkway, Markham
ON, L3R 4T8
www.reddeerpress.com
Published in the U.S. by Red Deer Press
311 Washington Street, Brighton,
Massachusetts 02135
Edited for the Press by Kathy Stinson
Cover image courtesy of iStockphoto & Shutterstock
Text design by Daniel Choi
Cover art by Richard Gokool

We acknowledge with thanks the Canada Council for the Arts, and the Ontario Arts Council for their support of our publishing program. We acknowledge the financial support of the Government of Canada through the Canada Book Fund (CBF) for our publishing activities.

ONTARIO ARTS COUNCIL
CONSEIL DES ARTS DE L'ONTARIO
50 YEARS OF ONTARIO GOVERNMENT SUPPORT OF THE ARTS
50 ANS DE SOUTIEN DU GOUVERNEMENT DE L'ONTARIO AUX ARTS

Canada Council
for the Arts
Conseil des Arts
du Canada

Library and Archives Canada Cataloguing in Publication
Terrell-Deutsch, Beverley, 1948-, author
Running scared / Beverley Terrell-Deutsch.
ISBN 978-0-88995-503-5 (pbk.)
I. Title.
PS8639.E774R85 2013   jC813.'6   C2013-904218-0
Publisher Cataloging-in-Publication Data (U.S.)
Terrell-Deutsch, Beverley.
Running scared / Beverley Terrell-Deutsch.
[168] p. : cm.
Summary: Gregory has a lot of fears – most of them as a result of the car accident that killed his dad. He uses a roundabout route to school to avoid the spot where the accident happened, but eventually he realizes that he has to confront his fears, by relying on his friends and his growing understanding that others have their own hangups.
ISBN: 978-0-88995-503-5 (pbk.)
1. Bullying – Juvenile fiction. 2. Teenagers and death – Juvenile fiction. 3. Parents – Death – Juvenile fiction. I. Title.
[Fic] dc23   PZ7.T374ru 2013
Printed and bound in Canada

ACKNOWLEDGMENTS

The author wishes to acknowledge the invaluable assistance of the following people:

Ted Staunton, without whose support and guidance, this book would never have existed; Kathy Stinson, whose editorial comments and wisdom provided the final shape for the book; Peter Carver and Richard Dionne; Anne Laurel Carter and Lee Gowan; and all my instructors at the University of Toronto School of Continuing Studies, Michael Winter, Elizabeth Ruth, Elaine Stirling, Kathy Kacer and especially Catherine Graham. Thanks are due, too, to early instructors at Humber College who helped set me firmly on the writing path, Nancy-Anne Purré, Eliza Clark and Carole Corbeil. And, of course, many thanks to Bob Deutsch for his ongoing help, enthusiasm and encouragement.

This book is dedicated to

my dear mom, Ruth Terrell (1917 – 2013),
who was always encouraging and so happy
when she heard this book was going to be published,

and to

Bob, my sweet husband and best friend.

ONE

No Way Around It

Gregory sat nervously tapping his pen against the desktop. He looked out the classroom window, watched the golden leaves drifting down, and wondered how to answer the first question. He had forgotten all about the science test. Oh, sure, he knew it was coming up soon. He just hadn't remembered it was today.

He looked down at his paper. Maybe if he wrote really carefully, Mr. Gladstone would give him some marks for neatness. It was worth a try. He started with his name; at least that much would be right. Then he tackled the first question.

Grade 6 Science Test

Name: *Gregory Gray*

Question 1: Describe the function of the human eye.

The human eye is in the human head. It is to see with. It can be blue or green or brown. There is a little black dot in the middle of it that is important. There are two of them ... not dots ... two eyes in each head.

Question 2: Describe three situations (A) in which you would need to protect your eyes, and (B) what you would do in each to provide that protection.

Gregory didn't like science. Last year's teacher had been short-tempered and boring. She made everything from science to language to social studies seem like drudgery. This year, Gregory had a teacher who was new to the school, Mr. Gladstone. So far, he seemed okay, but Gregory wasn't counting on it lasting.

Question 1 had started Gregory thinking ... humans

had two eyes, but what about animals that had just one eye? Didn't an octopus have just one big eye in the middle? And what about grasshoppers; didn't they have, like, a million eyes? Or was that flies? What would it be like, he wondered, having a million eyes? Wouldn't it be confusing? How would you decide which eye to look out of?

He pulled out his calculator, typed in 1,000,000, then multiplied it by 7.5. He already knew the answer, of course. But he loved 7.5. It was such a great-looking number. It was a tough number, too. It could stand up for itself. Gregory thought about 7.5 a lot.

7,500,000 flashed on the screen.

"And the square root would be ... hmmm," he pushed the square-root button ... "yes, I knew it ... 2738.6127, a nice easy number, the same at both ends. He flipped over his science test and, using the blank back page, began to play with numbers. Late last summer, almost by accident, he had discovered the weird relationship between odd numbers and squares. It was so perfect, he couldn't help running the pattern again. He grabbed his pen:

1 = 1 = 1 squared

1 + 3 = 4 = 2 squared

1 + 3 + 5 = 9 = 3 squared

$1 + 3 + 5 + 7 = ...$

"What are you doing, Gregory?"

Startled, Gregory looked up. It was Mr. Gladstone. He did not look happy.

"Nothing, sir," said Gregory.

"It doesn't look like nothing," said Mr. Gladstone, "but it doesn't look like your science test, either."

Some of the nearby students glanced over at Gregory, then bent dutifully back to their work. Only Teisha, a new girl who had only been at the school a few days, had a soft look on her face and kept on staring. Gregory was puzzling that over when Mr. Gladstone turned his paper right side up and tapped it firmly ... unmistakable teacher sign language for, "Get back to work, NOW."

Gregory looked over at Matt, his best friend since kindergarten. Matt had his shoulders hunched over his work, and Gregory could see that his page was full of tiny, tight writing. Gregory felt a little sick. He hadn't always been so awful at school. He used to be able to finish tests and get stuff done in between tests, too. Somehow, though, after the accident, all that had changed. Everything these days seemed to fizzle almost before it got started.

But numbers were different. Numbers were steady, reliable, unchanging. Numbers were his friends. They never let him down. He'd been thinking a lot about prime numbers lately: 2 was such a good number ... so were 3, 5, 7, and all the rest, but 2 was such a solid number. Meaningful. Not divisible without remainder by anything but itself and 1. Now 2 was not as nice as 7.5, but very nice, a great number, perfectly balanced and totally trustworthy.

"Gregory, you're still not working."

Gregory's head jerked up. It was Mr. Gladstone, who looked more puzzled now than annoyed. "I'd like you to stay behind at morning recess tomorrow for a few minutes," he said. "We need to talk."

"Yes, sir," said Gregory.

How did this happen? thought Gregory. I'm working on my test one minute, then all of a sudden, my brain is doing something completely different.

"Please write it in your Agenda so you won't forget."

"Yes, sir," repeated Gregory, but for the life of him, he couldn't think where his Agenda was.

Last thing that afternoon, without warning, a Special Assembly was called for the whole school. Unannounced Special Assemblies never happened.

"What's going on?" whispered Matt as the class made its way to the gym.

"I don't know," said Gregory. "Did somebody die?"

When they got to the gym, Gregory's class, as usual, sat cross-legged on the floor near the back. Assemblies were normally noisy, fun affairs, but today's was weirdly quiet. Gregory looked around. There were a lot of parents standing along the side walls or sitting on the benches at the back of the gym. What were they doing here? How did they find out about the Assembly? Parents only came to concerts and plays. Mrs. Clarkson, the school secretary, must have done a lot of quick phone calling and emailing this morning. The grown-ups all looked so serious. No one was chatting. No one was laughing. Even the babies in their strollers were quiet.

Mr. Sylvester, the principal, and then a white-haired man Gregory didn't recognize, walked to the center of the stage.

"Boys and girls, and parents," began Mr. Sylvester, "thank you for joining us today. I have a very important announcement to make. You may or may not know that for several months there have been discussions at the School Board about the possible closure of our school. We had hoped last June that the decision would be in our favor. However, the School Board met again last night and, despite everything we've done, including much input from our wonderful School Council, the decision has gone forward. As of January 1st, this school and two other small schools in this district will be closed. Students will be transferred to the new consolidated school being built in Richmond Hill, which will open in January."

Even though the announcement didn't seem to have much effect on the students, most of them did seem to get it that something sad, and even kind of tragic, was happening. The teachers and parents looked uniformly upset. Some of them looked angry, and some of them, including Mr. Gladstone, looked like they were going to cry. Gregory wondered whether he might be losing his job.

"This does not mean that we are giving up," said Mr. Sylvester. "Mr. Jacobson, Chairman of the School Council, will tell you now what we're planning to do to fight this decision."

The white-haired man approached the microphone. He told them how disappointed the School Council was about the Board's decision. He said that the loss of the local school would "detract significantly from the integrity of the community." He talked about "fighting back" and undertaking a "Save Our School" campaign. But after the first exciting bits about posters and petitions, Gregory's mind drifted off. For him, moving schools or staying at Centennial amounted to the same thing. School was school and he hated it, except for Math Club, of course. He loved Mr. Singh's Math Club. Tomorrow at lunch recess they were working on number patterns. He could hardly wait ...

"Gregory!" It was Matt motioning to him to get up. Everybody else was already standing, ready to file out of the gym. The assembly was over.

"I wonder what the letter says," said Matt on the way back to their classroom for dismissal.

"What letter?" said Gregory.

"You know, the letter we have to take home to our parents tonight, the letter Mr. Sylvester said was so important."

"Oh," said Gregory, "... that letter ..."

With the letter jammed into his backpack with his language homework, Gregory pushed open the big front doors of the school and started down the steps. He had glanced at the letter quickly when Mr. Gladstone handed them out, but it was all just the same stuff they had already heard about in the assembly.

Gregory was thinking so hard about the number of school days left in Grade 6 after today ... 278, including weekends and holidays ... 279 if it was a Leap Year, which it wasn't ... that he almost tripped over Teisha. She was sitting on the top step twirling a big, pointy, red and yellow leaf in her fingers.

"Isn't this pretty, Gregory?" she said. "I love autumn, don't you?"

"I guess so," said Gregory. He had barely noticed the leaves scattered across the lawn.

"Red and yellow and orange," said Teisha. "Fire colors."

"I guess so," said Gregory, wondering what this girl he hardly knew was talking about. He passed her on the steps then hurried down the school walkway toward the sidewalk.

"I thought I'd keep you company on the way home," said Teisha, carefully tucking the leaf in her pocket and coming down the steps behind him. "I usually walk with my little sister, but my *sobo*, my grandma, had to take her to the dentist. Do you know her? My sister, Tamara, I mean, not our dentist ... who isn't a woman, by the way, it's a man. But that doesn't matter.

My mother says that women probably make better dentists than men because their hands are smaller, but I've never thought much about it."

"You don't have to keep me company," Gregory said with a sinking feeling. "I go home a different way."

As usual, rather than turning right at the end of the school walkway and going a half-block past Mr. Yamamoto's Jiffy Mart and across the intersection at Henderson and Clarke, which would take him straight home, Gregory turned left. Of course, this route was much longer. He had figured, without actually measuring, that it was roughly four times the distance, and took him four times as long. Still, it was worth it. He didn't want to walk past the Jiffy Mart. But how could he explain that to anyone, especially this pushy girl he hardly knew? Why was she watching him walking home, anyway? Was she spying on him?

"I know you take the long way home," said Teisha. "I've seen you going this way, and I'm wondering why you do it?"

"It's just something I like to do," said Gregory with an even worse sinking feeling. He knew it was a lie and now felt doubly uncomfortable.

"Fine," she said. "I'll keep you company all the same."

They passed the school driveway and were on the

broken sidewalk that fronted the Centennial Woodlot. Teisha was stepping on all the uneven chunks of concrete like a tightrope walker. She held her arms out at her sides, balancing and placing her feet carefully, avoiding the gravelly parts like they were fire pits she might fall into any second.

What's the proportion of little bits of gravel to big chunks of concrete? thought Gregory. Would it be a constant, he wondered, or is it random? ...

"This is fun, Gregory," said Teisha, balancing on an extra big chunk. "You should try it."

They were walking past the big dead tree that leaned out over the sidewalk like a bench. Sometimes high school kids would hang out around the bench tree. Gregory always hurried past them. It was safer that way.

Today, a girl in a red dress was sitting there smoking. Her red fingernails contrasted sharply with the snow-white of the cigarette balanced between her fingers. Gregory had seen her here before, always alone and looking pretty scary.

"What are you staring at, Shrimp?" she snorted.

Quickly, he looked away and kept on walking, but Teisha stopped to confront the older girl.

"You should be smarter than that," he heard her say.

"They don't call them cancer sticks for nothing, you know."

Where does Teisha get the nerve? thought Gregory.

"Shut up and mind your own business, why don't you?!" The girl flicked the still burning butt straight at Teisha. Gregory gasped when he saw it flying through the air, trailing hot sparks, but Teisha neatly dodged it.

"Have it your way," Teisha said and ran to catch up with him.

"She's going to ruin her skin," she said, a little out of breath but not at all upset, "not to mention her lungs."

"What?" said Gregory.

"Smoking. It ruins your skin. Sucks all the collagen right out of it, that's what."

"Sounds like that might be a good thing," said Gregory, glad to have Teisha's attention on something other than why he took the long way home.

"Oh, no," said Teisha. "It's not a good thing at all. It leaves your skin, especially your neck and all around your eyes, like big empty bags of nothing. It's really, really disgusting. My mom knows all about this stuff. She's a nurse, you know."

"Gregory, wait up." It was Matt, skidding out of the school driveway on the Red Ripper, his 10-speed bike. Gregory stopped and watched him approach, riding fast, like he was in a race. He skidded to an expert, dust-swirling stop right beside them. Teisha gave a surprised yelp.

"What are you doing, Matt?" she said. "That's dangerous. You could have run us over. Besides, this is a busy street. There's lots of cars along here."

"Oh, dangerous, smangerous, Teisha. And I don't see any cars. Do you, Gregory?"

"No."

"See?" said Matt. "No cars."

"Well, there could be. Any second, there could be, and then you'd be in trouble."

Matt ignored her and addressed Gregory. "What's up? Where you guys going?"

Gregory began to feel exhausted. Now there were two of them questioning him. "I don't know what Teisha's doing," he said, "but I'm going home."

"I already told you, Gregory," said Teisha. "I want to know why you're going all this way around the block instead of going straight home with the rest of us."

"Well, maybe Gregory lives down here," said Matt.

Thanks Matt, thought Gregory. Good try.

"Oh, no, he doesn't live down here," said Teisha folding her arms. "Gregory lives four doors down from me in the townhouses. And you know it, Matt. You're over in the other section, but you live there, too."

"Well, and what if I do? So what?"

"So, Gregory doesn't live down here, and I want to know why he's walking this long, long way home, AND," she continued dramatically, "why he's walking the long way to school in the morning, too. I've seen you, Gregory. You leave really early. But then you're late for school a lot of the time. How come?"

"Teisha, I just like walking this way, that's all. Now, could you drop it?"

They were walking faster now, and Matt was trailing along on his bike. They were almost at the corner where Gregory would cross to Tiffen Close.

"Why should I drop it?" said Teisha. "I asked you a simple question."

"Just drop it," said Gregory.

"But, Gregory, it's so far. It must take you ages, especially in winter when the sidewalks are full of ice and snow. You must get really cold."

"I know you get cold," said Matt. "Remember when you got frostbite last winter?"

Gregory stared at him in surprise. He hadn't expected this. "Thanks a lot, Matt. I thought you were my friend."

"I am, Gregory, but you've got to admit it, your face was pretty frozen. You had to go to the doctor and everything. See, you've still got a little white mark there on your chin, a little scar."

"Just shut up. Shut up, the both of you."

"It's so silly," said Teisha. "You've got to have a reason."

Gregory couldn't take it anymore. "It's because I don't like walking past the Jiffy Mart. Okay? Are you satisfied? I DON'T like walking past the Jiffy Mart, so I walk the long way 'round. Now will you leave me alone?"

"But why, Gregory? Why don't you like walking past the Jiffy Mart? That's just silly."

"It is NOT silly," stammered Gregory. His face felt hot and suddenly his heart was racing.

"Yes, it is silly. It's very, very silly."

"It's where his dad died," said Matt in a voice so small Gregory barely heard it. "Now will you just shut up?"

"What?" said Teisha.

"Never mind," said Gregory. "It doesn't make any difference," and he turned and walked away.

"It's where his dad died," Gregory heard Matt explaining. "Last winter. It was a really bad ice storm, and there was a car accident right there in front of the Jiffy Mart, okay? That's why Gregory doesn't walk that way. Are you satisfied now?"

Teisha ran to catch up with Gregory. "I'm sorry," she said. "I didn't know about your dad. I'm really sorry."

"It's okay," said Gregory, but it wasn't.

"But you're going to have to go to the Jiffy Mart," said Teisha. "There's no way around it. You're going to have to go to the Jiffy Mart every day."

"What are you talking about?" said Gregory.

"Didn't you read the letter? For all us walkers, all the townhouse and Henderson Street kids, that's where the new school bus stop is going to be. Right there in front of the Jiffy Mart."

TWO

The Terrible Truth

Without looking, Gregory turned and ran across the street. A horn blared and brakes squealed. Behind him, Teisha yelled, "Are you crazy? You almost got hit by a car," but Gregory kept right on running, through Tiffen Close, through the public walkway, and past the red house where the big dog lived. He was a tawny yellow color with a big ruff of thick fur around his neck that made him look like a lion. Normally, Gregory forced himself to walk along here. Everyone knew the dog hated anyone running, that it made him even madder. But today, Gregory's head felt like it was going to explode.

The new bus stop. In front of the Jiffy Mart! It couldn't be. It just couldn't be.

Even though he was expecting it, when the dog came stampeding around the corner of the house, barking furiously, Gregory's heart leaped into his throat. The only thing separating them was a flimsy fence and twenty feet of empty roadway. Gregory's heart was pounding madly, but one part of his panic-stricken brain was coolly analyzing his problem. It was basically just another kind of mathematical equation in need of a solution: (New School) + (Bus Pick-up In Front Of Jiffy Mart) + (MUST Avoid Jiffy Mart) = x. Almost before he had formulated the question, the answer came. It was quite simple.

The minute Gregory opened his front door, he dumped his backpack and grabbed the phone. If he hadn't lost his cell phone in some snow bank last winter, he wouldn't have had to wait until he got home to make the call. But his mom had refused to buy him a replacement. "It's too expensive. You'll have to put up with using the house phone like I do until there's a bit more money around here." Since his dad had died, money had been a problem.

"Matt," said Gregory, still panting from his run,

"we've got to stop the school from closing." Chirp, Gregory's budgie, was screeching so loudly, he could hardly hear himself talk. Chirp wasn't used to being kept waiting in his cage. "Hang on ... I've got to let Chirp out." Gregory raced to the kitchen and opened the door of the cage. The little bird zoomed to the curtain rod above the kitchen window, then to the light fixture, then past Gregory into the front room. Gregory could hear him in there, singing his head off. Chirp loved being free.

Matt said, "I'm sorry about earlier. I shouldn't have said anything to Teisha about your dad. She's just so ... I don't know, so bossy or something. Anyway, I'm sorry."

"It's okay, Matt," said Gregory, "I'm sorry I got mad, too. And you were just telling her the truth. I don't think she would have quit until one of us told her. Maybe you did me a favor."

"I never saw you run so fast," said Matt. "I tried to follow you, but a bunch of cars came out of nowhere and I couldn't get across the street. By then, you were out of sight. You almost got hit by a car."

"Forget about that," said Gregory. "The important thing is we've got to stop the school from closing." He heard Matt take a bite of something.

"What are you eating?"

"A chocolate chip cookie."

"Well, chew quieter. What are we going to do? Maybe we should join the Save Our School thing."

"Yah, that sounds like a lot of fun," said Matt, clearly un-thrilled at the idea.

"Well, we've got to do something."

"I still don't get why you don't want to go to Jiffy Mart," said Matt. "I know your dad died there and everything, but why won't you go up there, even now? It was a long time ago, right?" In the background, Gregory could hear babies crying. Last summer, Matt's mother had had triplets, two girls and a boy. "Why don't you just get over the Jiffy Mart thing?"

"I could go up there if I WANTED to," said Gregory. "I just don't want to." There was still a big chunk missing from the concrete curb in front of the Jiffy Mart. Their car had smashed it off when the truck slid through the stop sign and hit them broadside. That gouge in the curb marked the spot where Gregory's dad had died. For the millionth time, he pushed away the image of his dad's face going so still and the memory of the awful silence after the crash.

"Let's just go up there," said Matt. "My mom asked me to go get some bread for supper. Come with me."

Matt made it sound so simple. He had always made it sound so simple, all the dozens of times he'd tried to convince Gregory to go up there with him. It wasn't simple, but maybe he should do it. Walk to the Jiffy Mart with Matt, buy some bread, then walk home again. It really was just walking up the street, no big deal. And Matt was right; the accident was a long time ago.

"Okay," said Gregory, with a little thrill of excitement. He was going to do it. "I'll meet you at the pillars in five minutes."

Gregory stood waiting for Matt at the crooked pillars that marked the entrance to the townhouse complex. But now that he was actually about to walk up to the Jiffy Mart, to go past the spot where his dad died, the feeling of excitement was gone. Instead, he felt goose bumpy all over. The sky was a bright autumn blue and the sun was warm, but still he shivered.

He was glad Matt hadn't suggested they ride their bikes. Gregory's bike, his beloved Green Hornet, seemed too fast now, too dangerous. What if a tire blew? What if he lost his balance?

Matt finally arrived, still eating chocolate chip cookies. He held one out to Gregory, but he shook his head. He felt a little sick as he turned his feet left toward Henderson.

"Have you started writing your Haiku poem yet for language tomorrow?" asked Matt around a mouthful. "I can't figure it out. I thought it would be easy, but it's not. Have you started yours?"

Gregory was having trouble listening to Matt. Every step brought them closer to the Jiffy Mart. Gregory could clearly see the cars up ahead, each one slowing and stopping, each one politely taking its turn going through the intersection. And there, on the other side of the big red mailboxes, was where it had happened.

"Well, have you?"

"No," muttered Gregory.

"Me neither. What is a syllable, anyway, and why does there have to be five of them in a line? Or is it seven in a line? Or is it five in one line and seven in the next one?"

Matt chattered on about Haiku as they got closer and closer to the Jiffy Mart, and then about his favorite movies. He told Gregory again about his dad's new projector TV and the big 100-inch screen that came down right out of the ceiling. Gregory and Matt had watched movies at Matt's house nearly every Friday night for as long as Gregory could remember. The huge new screen sounded awesome. But, try as he might,

Gregory couldn't concentrate. His heart was beating fast. His head buzzed, full of the sounds of squealing brakes and shattering glass, the smell of burning rubber. And then he could see the spot, that awful gash in the curb, and his knees began to shake. It wasn't that he didn't want to go up to the Jiffy Mart. He couldn't.

"... I think he's the greatest, don't you, and he does his own stunts and everything."

"I've gotta go." Gregory turned and ran as fast as his wobbly legs would carry him, back home, away from the Jiffy Mart and all that had happened there.

THREE

Number Pattern Puzzles

Matt caught up with him at the pillars. "Guess that didn't work."

"Guess not," said Gregory. "I don't think anything will work. That's why we've got to stop the school from closing. We've got to join the Save Our School campaign."

"Okay," said Matt. "Let's find out more about it tomorrow. But I gotta go get the bread. Mom will be wondering what's taking me so long."

Gregory walked slowly down the sidewalk and up the steps to his front door. He let himself in, then, with his fingers still shaking, let Chirp out of his cage again.

The little bird flew up to the kitchen curtain rod. He stayed there, singing and talking his budgie-talk as if nothing was the matter.

When he was steady enough, Gregory changed the papers in the bottom of Chirp's cage, filled the food dish with pellets, then cleaned and refilled the water bowl. With a sigh, he sat down at the kitchen table, took a pencil from the empty jam jar in the middle, and began making up math puzzles. Math Club was tomorrow. Mr. Singh had said they'd be working on number pattern puzzles. Each student was supposed to bring at least two, and everybody would try to solve everyone else's puzzles.

Gregory started with a number pattern that wasn't too hard, something easy to get going:

1, 3, 7, 13, 21, ___. Adding consecutive even numbers to each item was pretty easy ... $1 + 2 = 3$; $3 + 4 = 7$; $7 + 6 = 13$; $13 + 8 = 21$. It was easy to figure out the next number in the series ... 21 plus 10 and the answer was 31. Simple.

Then he tried it using consecutive odd numbers: 1, 2, 5, 10, 17, ___. That was pretty easy, too.

Then he set a more difficult one. He smiled. It had a little twist. A nice little surprise right in the middle: 1, 2, 4, 7, 11, 14, 16, ___.

It was getting late, so he decided it was time to quit. His mom would be home soon, and he'd have to start helping get supper ready. On the back of the page, he wrote down the answers to the three puzzles: 31, 26, and 17. Mr. Singh had insisted that they provide the answers and be prepared to explain the rationale for the pattern.

"We can learn from problems in mathematics," said Mr. Singh, "but only if we know and understand both the problem and the solution." He had emphasized the understand part.

That reminded him. Two days after she had arrived at the school, Teisha had joined the Math Club. Gregory couldn't figure out why. She didn't seem to like numbers all that much and wasn't even very good with them. At her very first Math Club meeting, she had sat in a desk beside Gregory and asked him all kinds of questions. Once he explained things, she generally understood, but it didn't seem to be all that much fun for her.

The front door opened. His mom walked in, looking tired and grimy from the studio. She tossed her jacket on the back of a chair and stood looking at him.

"Are you all right?" she said.

"Yes."

"You look terrible, Gregory. Like the stuffing has been knocked out of you. What is it? Has something happened?"

"No, Mom. I'm okay," he said, "but we found out today that the school might be closing. There's a letter here all about it. Mr. Sylvester says we're going to have a Save Our School campaign. I think I'll join. Matt, too."

She picked up the letter. "Sounds serious. I think it'd be great for you to join the campaign ... if you want to ..." and she gave him a questioning look. He knew she was wondering at his sudden interest in anything to do with school.

A thousand times Gregory had wanted to tell his mom about the Jiffy Mart, but he couldn't. At first, he didn't think it was important. But as time went on, and he was still taking the long route, it seemed impossible to bring it up. It was strange, like somehow he had missed his chance. And how could he possibly explain it to her now?

"Let me know if there's anything I can do to help," his mom said and crossed to the sink to wash her hands and arms, right up to her elbows. "Artists can come in handy sometimes ... you know, with flyers or posters, that kind of thing." She turned on the taps. The water ran blue from the paint. She was painting a winter skyscape for the Canadian Opera Company. They were doing something in Italian, she'd said, something about a guy who lives in a loft whose girlfriend has cold hands.

"That sky," she said, "it goes on forever, and the sink is backed up again at work. Can you believe it?"

"When will it be finished, do you think?" asked Gregory. He started to set the table ... knives, forks, spoons, napkins, glasses ... Since his dad had died, Gregory tried to help out around the house like his dad used to.

"Probably never," she answered, scrubbing at her face with a wet towel. Then she turned to the sink to mop up the mess she'd made. "It goes on and on and on. There's acres of it. She threw down the towel, stepped across the space between sink and refrigerator, and yanked open the freezer door. "What do you want for dinner, maestro? I made up some meat patties yesterday. Sound any good?"

"Yes," he said. "Perfect."

"Great. You make us a salad. I'm going for my run. Just 3K tonight. I'm wiped. Be back in fifteen minutes ... where did I leave my iPod?"

"Do you have to run every night?" said Gregory.

"Gregory, since your dad died, I've had to work really

hard to make ends meet. I'm not complaining; I love my job. But I've got to do something fun, too. This is my fun; it makes me feel good. Some day, when I'm good enough, I'm going to run a marathon ... well, maybe a half-marathon to start. Why don't you train with me? I know you'd be a great runner."

"No, thanks."

Since his dad died, Gregory knew his mom had to work hard to pay all the bills. But it seemed now that all she did was go to work and then come home and run.

In a strange way, though, that was exactly what Gregory wanted. If she was out running, she wasn't asking questions, wasn't trying to get him to talk. Sure, they talked about dad and how hard it was without him and how much they missed him. They even talked about the accident and that awful night. But for Gregory, it was always on the surface. He didn't let himself go too deep into his feelings, not like his mom. She went plenty deep. But Gregory didn't. Talking about it, deep-talking about it, would make it real in some crazy way. If he didn't do that, then his dad wasn't really gone. He was still alive and big and could walk in the door at any minute.

Later, after supper, Gregory decided he should tell his

mom about the science test, but when he looked up from his homework, she was asleep. Her head was leaned back against the sofa cushions and her feet were stretched out on the coffee table. He looked up at the wall above her head. A framed poster she had painted used to hang there: "In Everything Give Thanks." Now there was just an empty nail hole and a faint outline on the wallpaper where it had been.

Gregory's dad had been the minister at Central Church. There were lots of posters his mom had painted in the church hallways and Sunday School rooms and around the house, too. "Do unto others as you would have them do unto you." "Love is Kind. Love is Patient. Love Never Fails." But when his dad died, his mom had put "In Everything Give Thanks" in the basement. "I can't look at it, Gregory," she'd said. "It used to make sense to me, but now it doesn't."

Gradually, over the past year, though friends and acquaintances and even the new minister from the church had tried hard, Gregory's mom had refused to return to services. Gradually, the visits and phone calls, the casseroles and little note cards dwindled away. Only Mrs. Summer, Gregory's Sunday School teacher, stayed in touch. She called every week or so, kept Gregory's mom informed about church news, and always invited them to come back, even for a visit.

But Gregory's mom was immovable and, gradually, mealtime grace and bedtime prayers disappeared, too. Now their home had a strange, empty feel that had nothing to do with, but everything to do with his father's death.

FOUR

Dead Daisies

Tuesday morning was sunny and hot. Except for all the red and yellow trees that used to be green, it could have been summer. How many leaves are on that tree? The question suddenly inserted itself into Gregory's brain. Would there be a million? He realized with a little shock that, though he had been looking at trees his entire life, he had no idea, NO IDEA how many leaves might be on one of them. How weird was that! But how would you count the leaves on a tree?

Would you take one branch, count the leaves on it, then count the number of branches and multiply? That would be such a rough estimate, though. No, that wouldn't work. Weigh the tree with and without leaves, weigh one leaf and divide? Too difficult, and you'd have to cut the tree down to weigh it.

Gregory realized he'd been standing, thinking about the leaf problem rather than getting to school. This morning, of all mornings, he didn't want to be late. The first planning meeting for the Save Our School campaign was at 8:30 and he had to be there. Besides, he'd already been late for school four times, and he knew from experience that five times late meant an automatic detention.

He ran down his front steps, cut across the tiny lawn to the sidewalk, and hurried past Teisha's house.

"Hi, Gregory."

"Hi, Tamara." It was Teisha's little sister, sitting on her front steps, eating a bowl of cereal. He hoped he wouldn't see Teisha. He was still angry with her for being so nosey and pushy yesterday. He felt ashamed, too, at having run away.

"What do you call a grizzly bear with no teeth?" Tamara called out to him as he passed. He pretended he hadn't heard, but she persisted. "Gregory, what do you call a grizzly bear ..."

"I don't know," he shouted over his shoulder.

"A gummy bear, silly."

He picked up his pace. Just the way she'd said "silly" irritated him. She sounded just like Teisha.

He was practically running out through the crooked pillars when he noticed a dead daisy lying in the middle of the sidewalk. It seemed an odd, sad little sight. Gregory hurried on.

Then, once again, placed exactly in the middle of the sidewalk, lay another dead daisy. Its head pointed in the same direction as the first one. Gregory stopped and looked around. Nobody in sight. He kept walking. A few steps further on was another daisy, just like the first two. One dead daisy meant nothing, two was a little strange, but three daisies just lying there by accident was definitely a mathematical improbability. And all three of them were pointed in the same direction, westward toward Henderson Street. This was no random event. This was obviously a trail.

Gregory followed it, going the other direction, back toward its source. He certainly wasn't going to follow the trail up toward the Jiffy Mart. Further along was a fourth dead daisy and, a little further still, a fifth. It continued like this all the way down to Simcoe Street. It was here that Gregory should turn left to go to school.

But the trail of dead daisies continued straight on into Sprucewood Lane. Gregory had never been down Sprucewood Lane.

He stood there, undecided. He shifted his backpack, felt his fingers tightening on the straps. He wanted to follow the trail, to solve the problem of the dead daisies. Who had put them there, and why? Mr. Singh always said, never be afraid of a problem. "All learning occurs in the solving of problems," he said. But Sprucewood Lane was creepy. The road was lined with giant spruce trees so thick you couldn't see what lay behind them, and so old their bottom branches reached out and brushed the edge of the sidewalk.

The sudden startled squawk of a crow, sitting like a demented Christmas angel at the top of one of the spruces, made up Gregory's mind for him. He turned and ran for school.

As his foot hit the school walkway, the bell rang for classes to begin. Not only had he missed the meeting, he was late for school.

Mrs. Clarkson, the school secretary, looked sympathetic when she handed him the pink Late Slip and the blue Detention Slip. "I'm sorry, Gregory," she said. "Maybe if you got to bed earlier, you wouldn't be late for school so often. Don't forget, detention at lunch recess today. Room 7."

That morning, Mr. Gladstone gave the class back their science tests. Gregory was disappointed and embarrassed when he saw his failing grade, 3 out of 25 ... 12%. Quickly, he shoved the test into his backpack before anyone else could see that big blue 3. At least Mr. Gladstone didn't use red ink. Failing in red ink seemed so much worse than failing in blue ink.

Gregory was on his way out the door for morning recess, when Mr. Gladstone said, "Please stay behind, Gregory."

Gregory knew he deserved a lecture about the science test. He'd never even studied for it. Why hadn't he? He'd been planning to. But like so many things in Gregory's life lately, what he planned to do, and what he actually did were two very different things.

"Thanks, Gregory, for staying behind. I want to ask you a couple of questions. I'm actually pretty confused."

"You are?"

"Yes, I am. I think you're a smart boy, Gregory. You're never a disturbance in class. You seem to be working. You seem to want to do well, want to apply yourself, but then you end up having difficulty."

"I know. I did terrible on the science test."

"Gregory, it's not just science. You're doing poorly in social studies and language arts, too."

Gregory had the familiar sinking feeling, that empty, hollow feeling that nothing was right and nothing would ever be right. "I'm sorry, Mr. Gladstone."

"The only thing you're doing well in, in fact, really well in, exceptionally well in, is math."

"I like math."

"I know you do. I had a look at the math work you were doing on the back of your science test. To tell you the truth, Gregory, I couldn't quite figure out what those lists of numbers meant. Can you explain it to me?"

Gregory went to his desk, grabbed his backpack and hauled out the crumpled test paper. Mr. Gladstone turned it over and flattened it out. He pointed to the first column of numbers. "What's this, Gregory? It looks like some kind of a number pattern."

Mr. Gladstone was interested in the relationship between odd numbers and squares, too. Gregory's heart leaped up.

"It is," he said, pointing to the first line. "That's exactly what it is. A number pattern. Last summer, I was playing around with some odd numbers, and then I started organizing them and then squaring them. I was looking at the square roots, too, though none of them, by definition, has a square root. I was just playing around, doing all sorts of things, you know ..." Gregory could hear the excitement in his voice as he continued to explain. "And then I saw this pattern. See? $1 + 3 = 4 = 2$ squared, and next, $1 + 3 + 5 = 9 = 3$ squared. See? The pattern goes on forever, to infinity. You add up sequences of odd numbers, and then you find that the answers are also a sequence, an exact sequence of numbers that are themselves squares. Isn't it cool?"

"Yes, now I see," said Mr. Gladstone, and he smiled up at Gregory. "I never would have figured it out. This is amazing. I think you have a special talent with numbers."

"Oh, I just like numbers, that's all," said Gregory. "Numbers never change."

"Numbers are reliable. Is that it?"

"YES," said Gregory. Mr. Gladstone ... he understood! "No matter who looks at them, or whatever happens, numbers are solid. They don't change. You can count on them."

"Literally," said Mr. Gladstone with a smile.

Gregory laughed. It felt good, and surprising, to laugh.

"Gregory, why do you think you're such a brilliant student in math, but you're doing so poorly in your other subjects? Do you have any idea what's going on?"

Tears welled suddenly in Gregory's eyes. How could he tell his teacher what it felt like to lose his father the way he had? How he'd tried to block out the awful details of that night but, again and again, they just kept flooding back.

At first, with the blinding white brilliance of the exploding airbags, it had flashed through Gregory's mind that this must be heaven. He must be dead. But he hadn't felt anything. No pain. Then his father moaned beside him and Gregory knew this wasn't heaven. His father was still sitting behind the steering wheel, but the car door and window on that side of the car were smashed in. His father was leaning back against the headrest, his eyelids fluttering like two dark moths. There was blood on his face.

"Dad! Dad!"

Light from the Jiffy Mart window poured in through the demolished windshield and Mr. Yamamoto, inside the shop, stared out at the wreck that had smashed its way from the intersection into his parking lot.

"Dad! Dad!"

Wind gusted through the car's broken windows. Snowflakes swirled silently in the bright beam of the spotlight on the corner of the building. Gregory tried to move but his seatbelt held him tight. Mr. Yamamoto came out and tried to open Gregory's door, but it was buckled and wouldn't budge. Mrs. Yamamoto brought out a blanket and pushed it through the broken window, trying to tuck it in around Gregory without making any more of the glass fall in on him. She had talked to him, he remembered, but he didn't hear her, not one word.

It was then that Gregory noticed his dad was very still.

"DAD!!!"

"That's okay, Gregory," Mr. Gladstone said. "We can talk another time." He handed Gregory back his science test. "You go on out for recess now. Thanks for explaining the number pattern to me. I think it's terrific."

FIVE

Fight, Fight, Fight

At lunch, Gregory, Matt, and Teisha sat together. As usual, tables had been set up in the gym for students who didn't go home to eat. Even though his sandwich was his favorite, peanut butter and banana, he couldn't eat it. Matt ate his own lunch, then finished off Gregory's.

Teisha, who usually talked like she was afraid she'd run out of words if she ever stopped, was unusually quiet. Finally, she looked over at him and said, "I'm really sorry, Gregory, for upsetting you yesterday."

It seemed she could read his mind. He'd just been

thinking about that. "It's okay," he said.

"No, it isn't. You almost got hit by a car. I know sometimes I'm a pain. My mom's always yelling at me. She says, 'Nobody likes a Miss Bossy Pants,' but I can't help it. I try not to be bossy, but it's no use." Teisha sighed. "I'm sorry, too, about your dad. It must be really hard walking the long way 'round to school. I think you must be really brave."

It was the last thing Gregory expected to hear. He wasn't brave. If ever there was a coward, he was it.

"But I've got a plan for you," Teisha said.

"What plan?" said Gregory and Matt together.

"I'm not telling, not yet." She looked so smug, Gregory was almost annoyed with her all over again. It was hard to be mad at her, though, when she smiled at him like that.

"And," she said, "I've got a plan for the Save Our School campaign, too. I was hoping at least one of you would show up for the meeting this morning," and she glanced at Gregory. "There were lots of teachers there but only about ten kids, mostly Grade 7's and 8's. I can't believe the student apathy around here."

"The what?" said Matt.

"Student apathy," repeated Teisha, louder than she

needed to. "It means when kids don't care about stuff like this and refuse to get involved."

"I meant to be there, really I did," said Gregory. "I thought I left early enough, but then I saw this trail of dead daisies and I followed it down to Sprucewood Lane ..."

"A trail of what?" said Matt.

"Dead daisies."

"A trail of dead daisies?" said Teisha.

"Yes. It was the weirdest thing. I almost forgot to tell you. Someone left a trail of them all along Clarke Street. It went from Sprucewood Lane as far up toward Henderson as I could see."

"Why would anyone leave a trail of daisies?" Teisha said. "It's kind of creepy. Like Hansel and Gretel or something."

"Yah," said Matt, "Hansel and Gretel. Creepy with a capital CREEP ..."

"You mean, 'creepy with a capital C,'" said Teisha.

"Oh, get over yourself, Teisha," said Matt. "It sounds cool, Gregory. Like a real mystery. Maybe there's a gang of thieves or something, giving signals to each other."

Teisha gave him a glance but didn't say anything. "It is very strange, Gregory. What do you think? Should we follow the trail? Find out where it leads? I wonder who made it and why?"

"The trail led up toward the Jiffy Mart, right?" said Matt.

"I think so. I don't know," said Gregory. "It went as far up Clarke as I could see. It might have led to the Jiffy Mart. It might have gone further. Didn't you guys notice them on your way to school?"

"No," said Teisha.

"Neither did I," said Matt, "but I wasn't really looking for anything like that."

"How could anybody be looking for something like that?" said Teisha with a scowl.

"Forget it," said Gregory. It seemed Matt and Teisha would argue at the slightest opportunity. "The daisies aren't the important thing right now. The important thing is making sure the school doesn't close. What happened at the planning meeting, Teisha? What did they say?"

"We've decided to have 'Save Our School' signs printed up on hard plastic so the rain won't wreck them, but it's expensive," she said. "The School Council is going to pay for one hundred of them. Mr. Sylvester is going to order them today, and it'll take a few days to get them printed. I suggested we paint some signs ourselves, too. I said it would show student industry. The teachers seemed to like that."

"My mom said she'd help," said Gregory. "She'll paint some big posters that we can hang up in the library or maybe some of the stores."

"Your mom's an artist?" said Teisha.

"Yes."

"My mom's a nurse," she said.

"Like you haven't told us that a million times already," said Matt.

"Well, it's true," said Teisha, "and I'm glad your mother's an artist, Gregory. I think we should get her to paint an extra big poster and hang it up in the Jiffy Mart. Everybody from around here goes in there sooner or later. It would be great advertising for the campaign."

"Right," said Gregory. It certainly wouldn't be him placing that poster.

"We're also planning a parent information meeting for Friday night. Do you think you and your mom can come, Gregory? What about your parents, Matt? Everybody is supposed to help with this."

"Yes," said Gregory, "I think we can come."

"But what about our movie night?" said Matt.

"Oh," said Gregory, "I forgot. But we've got to fight

the school closing. Could we see the movie Saturday night instead?"

"I'll ask my dad," said Matt, "but I know my parents are way too busy with the babies to go to the meeting. Our house is like a zoo."

"Want to come with my mom and me?" said Gregory.

"No. It'll probably be boring, anyway."

"It will NOT be boring," said Teisha. "It'll be important, that's what it'll be."

"Why do you care so much about the school closing anyway, Teisha?" said Matt. "You hardly even know it yet. Not like Gregory and me. We've gone here ever since kindergarten."

Teisha crumpled her sandwich wrapper and opened a bag of Cheezies. She offered one to Gregory. He shook his head. "You're right," she said, "but I'm so tired of changing schools. Tamara and I have had three moves in the past two years and I like this school. I really like this school." She looked at Gregory.

"Are you sure you don't want a Cheezie?"

He shook his head.

"Could I have one?" asked Matt, and she handed him the rest of the bag.

The bell rang, signaling students they could proceed outdoors for the rest of lunch recess. Gregory pushed his chair back and stood up. "We've got to do what Mr. Sylvester suggested," he said. "We've got to get people to put those signs on their lawns. We've got to get lots of people to sign the petition, too. If enough people get together to try to stop it, maybe the School Board will change its mind and the school won't close."

"Yah," said Matt, licking his orange fingers and following Gregory out of the gym. "It sounds like fun. We're gonna fight the closing. Fight, fight, fight," and he punched the air. "Yay, team!"

Teisha frowned. "It's not some silly ball game. This is serious."

"I know," said Matt, "but just because it's serious doesn't mean it can't be fun. Right, Gregory?" and the boys grinned at each other.

"As soon as the signs and the petition forms are available, we'll get started," Teisha said. "We should be fully operational by Friday."

"Fully operational," said Matt, mimicking Teisha in a sing-songy voice, and he and Gregory laughed.

"I don't see what's so funny," said Teisha.

Matt headed outside to play soccer, and Gregory hurried down the hall toward Mr. Singh's classroom.

But with every step came a nagging feeling he had forgotten something. Something really important. He tried to chase it around inside his head, but it was impossible, like trying to find the end of a Moebius Loop.

SIX

Math Club Meeting

At Math Club, Teisha set a number pattern no one could solve, not Gregory, not even Mr. Singh. They finally put it aside for people to work on and bring back to Friday's meeting.

Gregory worked hard to solve Teisha's puzzle, but he had never seen anything like it. He just couldn't crack the code. Privately, he began to wonder whether she had made a mistake in her sequence. Or, and he didn't want to think this, maybe she had just made up a sequence of random numbers and there was no solution. It made him uncomfortable to think about it, but the thought lodged in his brain and he couldn't shake it out.

Finally, he decided it was too noisy in the Club meeting to concentrate, and his mind kept flipping back to "fight, fight, fight" anyway. In some ways, Gregory didn't want to fight. He didn't want to even have to think about the school closure. But he had to help stop it. Still, how was he going to do that? His brain jumped back and forth between consternation and resentment at his predicament, then, next thing he knew, he was thinking about Teisha's number pattern, 0, 1, 8, 11, 88, 101, __. It was enough—all of it—to make him dizzy.

He would work on it at home. It was quieter there. It was a tough one, for sure. He had never seen zero used as a starting point.

"Give up?" said Teisha, looking over his shoulder at the different solutions he had tried.

"No, not yet. I'll work on it some more at home," he said, and tore the sheet out of his workbook and shoved it into his pocket. "Did you solve any of mine?"

"No. Are you kidding? They're way too hard."

"Well, I can explain them for you, if you'd like."

"No." Teisha shoved her chin up with a mulish look on her face. "That would be cheating. I want to not get them on my own, fair and square."

When Gregory got home from school that afternoon, Chirp enjoyed shoulder time, chirping and preening, while Gregory cleaned out his cage. All the while, Gregory was trying to push thoughts of the school closure and the Jiffy Mart bus stop from his mind.

Chirp squawked, demanding Gregory's attention. He knew what his little pet wanted. That bird was just too smart for his own good.

Gregory went to the fridge, took three blueberries from the box on the top shelf, washed them, and set them on the table. Chirp flew down from the curtain rod, snatched one in his beak, and devoured it. Two seconds later, the other blueberries were history, too. Blueberries were Chirp's new favorite treat. He walked up Gregory's arm and began to nibble his ear, begging for more. Gregory got him two more berries from the fridge, already dreading the clean-up of "blue poo," and sat down at the kitchen table.

He forced his mind away from the bus stop problem and began to think about Teisha's number pattern instead. He pulled the crumpled paper from his pocket and looked at it again. Why couldn't he figure it out? He hoped she wasn't playing some kind of a trick. Again, his mind circled back to the possibility that she had just written down a sequence of random numbers to which there was no pattern, no real solution. That's what she could say, he thought. "That's the answer. There is no answer."

If that was the case, Gregory had to hand it to her, she had fooled everyone and, in a sense, it was kind of clever and kind of funny. But, basically, if it wasn't a number pattern, and that was what the task had been, then it wasn't honest. Again, he reasoned, she could counter, "That's the pattern, that there isn't any pattern." But he knew he'd be disappointed in her if that's what she said Friday when she presented the solution. Numbers weren't for telling lies or doing cheap tricks.

He smoothed out the paper, grabbed his purple pencil and began to work in earnest: 0, 1, 8, 11, 88, 101, ___. There was that zero ... strange ... Maybe clever. Maybe not. The pattern was not in the difference between the numbers. It wasn't squares or square roots of progressions. It wasn't multiples or anything else he could think of.

Could it be a phone number, a long distance, maybe European or Asian number? That would definitely be cheating. Again, he could hear Teisha arguing, "Of course, it's a number pattern. A very particular number pattern. It's the unique pattern of someone's phone number. How can you say that isn't a pattern?"

Gregory had always done this, been able to argue an opponent's point of view better than he could argue his own. It was discouraging and always left him feeling deflated, like he could never be right. But numbers WERE either right or wrong. Always. There was no in-between with numbers. No amount of arguing would change a wrong number into a right one, or a right number into a wrong one. That was one of the great things about numbers, one of the things that Gregory loved.

He stared at Teisha's number puzzle, making his mind a blank, letting his unconscious brain analyze the pattern without himself interfering with the process.

Nothing!

This rarely happened to Gregory, and when it did, there was always a way to find the solution, either through a textbook or on the Internet or by discussing it with Mr. Singh.

Finally, Gregory gave up. After all that hard work, he was getting hungry. He checked his watch. His mom wouldn't be home for another hour.

He pulled the toaster out of the cupboard and plugged it in. He grabbed two pieces of thick, crusty bread from the fridge. He shoved down the little handle and saw the elements inside go red. For once, it hadn't stuck. The toaster was getting old and sometimes didn't work quite right.

Gregory sat back down at the table. He had a few minutes. Maybe working on prime numbers would settle his mind, get him thinking about something other than Teisha's wonky puzzle and the school closure.

He grabbed a fresh pencil and wrote down the first thirty prime numbers from memory. That brought him up to 113. He knew that the further you went, the more rare and difficult to recognize they became ... 127 ... 131 ... He could easily look them all up on the Internet, but he wanted to figure them out for himself. No one had ever discovered a pattern for identifying prime numbers, but Gregory was sure there had to be one, and someday someone would find it.

Gregory smelled something burning. He looked up from his work to see the air above the toaster turning black with smoke. Chirp shrieked and flew to the front room.

The toaster was on fire! The little handle on the toaster had melted and bright yellow flames shot straight up out of the double slots. Nothing was left of the toast but two black lumps.

Gregory jumped up. Careful not to burn himself, he pulled out the plug. The fire didn't stop. Smoke continued to spiral heavily upward. The ceiling alarm began to blare. Gregory was coughing now and the smell of burnt bread and melting plastic was making it hard to breathe. He ran and threw all the downstairs windows open. When he returned to the kitchen, the fire was licking up the outside of the toaster from underneath.

Using the unplugged cord as a kind of leash, Gregory dragged the burning mess to the edge of the sink and toppled it in. He reached over and turned on the tap, full blast. With an angry sizzle and an upward rush of hot steam and black smoke, the fire died. Gregory grabbed a tea towel and flapped it at the smoke until he thought his arms would fall off.

Finally, the air cleared. The alarm stopped.

As he reached up to close the last window in the front room, Gregory noticed the screen. It was loose, hanging open by one hook, swinging lazily in the evening breeze. How did that happen? When did it get broken? And then a new thought struck Gregory. Where's Chirp?

SEVEN

37.0

Gregory ran through the house, calling for Chirp, but there was no answer. Just quiet and darkness slowly gathering in the corners as day dipped toward night. He ran outside.

"Chirp, Chirp," he called, running first down the sidewalk toward Matt's, then, when there was no sign of the bird, running back up the other way. Nothing. He hardly knew where to look. Chirp had never been outside before. Sure, free inside the house, almost all the time they were at home, but never free outside. Gregory felt the cold edge of panic gripping him. Where could Chirp be?

"Oh, God! Oh, God! Oh, God!" shouted Gregory.

"Just quit your swearing, why don't you? It's pretty rude."

It was Teisha, standing out in front of her house, yelling at him. Would this pushy, bossy girl never leave him alone?

"I'm NOT swearing," he yelled back. "I'm praying. My father was a minister, you know, and my budgie is gone, and I don't know where he is. I don't even know where to start looking."

"Well, I think you can quit both your praying and your looking." Teisha walked down the sidewalk toward Gregory, and sitting on her shoulder, as calm as could be, was a small green bird.

"Chirp!" Gregory ran toward her and took the bird in his hands. "Where did you find him?"

"I didn't find him. He found me," said Teisha. "Dad dropped us off; he took us out to dinner at Swiss Chalet. We're supposed to be with him this week, but he's 'overwhelmed at work' again, as usual. So we're with Mom instead. He's an accountant, you know. He works with numbers all day long, but I don't think he likes them, not like you, Gregory. Anyway, his cell phone rings all the time, and Tamara and I, we never know whether we're staying or going. I think the Swiss

Chalet tonight was because he feels guilty."

Gregory couldn't follow all the convolutions of Teisha's explanation, and didn't care to. "But how did Chirp find you?" he said, stroking the soft feathers on the bird's little head over and over again and blinking back his tears.

"Chirp, that's a cute name," said Teisha, and reached out to stroke him, too. "I don't know how he found me. Tamara had already gone inside and I was just standing there, waving goodbye to my dad. I saw him flying around ... the bird, not my dad. That would be really silly. Anyway, I didn't think he was a normal bird. You know, I thought he must be something special, someone's pet or something, and I thought he looked a little scared. So I just stood there, really still, and he came and lighted right on my shoulder."

"Thanks, Teisha. Thanks a lot." They'd been slowly walking toward Gregory's house as they talked. At the walkway leading to his front door, he suddenly felt awkward, not sure what to do next. Somehow he wanted to show his gratitude. "Want to come in?" he said. "My mom's not home from work yet, but you could come in, if you like. You could . . . you could ... see Chirp's cage." As soon as he said it, he knew it was a dumb thing to say. He felt his face go red.

"Thanks, Gregory," said Teisha with a grin. "I've got to go, but I'll take a rain check. My *sobo* is expecting me. I've got to help Tamara with her reading. She hasn't a clue."

"Okay," said Gregory, wondering what a rain check was. "Thanks again for saving Chirp," and he turned and ran up his front steps.

He was just shutting the door when Teisha called his name. "I like 37.0."

"What?"

She cupped her hands around her mouth like a megaphone and shouted. "I like the number 37.0. I heard you say you like 7.5. Well, I like 37.0."

"37.0? Why?"

"I'll give you a hint," she called. "My mom's a nurse."

"I know," said Gregory. "What's that got to do with it?"

But Teisha was already gone.

EIGHT

Stand-off

The next day after lunch, just as he and Matt were heading outside to play soccer, Gregory felt a tap on his shoulder. It was Mrs. Checklee, the Detention Room teacher. She was standing there with big black question marks in her eyes.

"Aren't you forgetting something, Mr. Gray?" she said. With a sinking feeling, Gregory realized he'd forgotten all about yesterday's detention and gone to Math Club instead.

"I'm sorry, Mrs. Checklee."

"Too late for 'sorry' now, my friend. You'll have to serve yesterday's detention today, and then you'll have another detention tomorrow as punishment for the missed one. You know that, Gregory. Now, go get your Detention Slip and meet me in Room 7 along with the rest of the miserable crew."

On his way home that afternoon, Gregory pulled his jacket tighter around him and glanced up at the sky. The sun, so warm and bright that morning, had disappeared behind a sky of lumpy black clouds. A damp wind had picked up. Leaves swirled through the air. The sidewalks and grassy verges were covered with them.

Gregory crossed Simcoe Street, dreading, as usual, the sudden rush of the big yellow lion-dog. But it was nowhere in sight. Then he saw why. The fence, over at the far corner, that flimsy fence, was crushed and trampled down. The dog was gone. He's loose, thought Gregory, and his heart began to thump. In his imagination, the dog's long white fangs grew to ten times their size, and he could almost feel them sinking in.

Gregory started walking fast. He wanted to run, but he was afraid to, knowing the effect running had on the dog. If he was anywhere around, that would surely make it so much worse. Walking as fast as he could, occasionally tripping over his own feet, Gregory reached the corner. Even though he was no safer there than when he'd been standing across the street from where the dog lived, he felt safer because he was on Clarke Street. He was almost home.

It was then that he heard barking and yells, yells that turned into terrified screams; they were coming from the townhouse complex. Gregory ran toward the sound, his backpack pounding against his shoulders with every step. He rounded the entrance pillars and saw the big dog ahead of him, running full-speed up the middle of the road. Further on, twenty paces ahead, were Teisha and Tamara, running away and screaming in fear. Even as he watched, Tamara tripped and fell headlong onto the road, the rough tarmac raking her bare knees and hands. Teisha stopped to help her sister and was screaming, half-dragging the younger girl to her feet, trying to run backward away from the dog.

Gregory skidded to a stop. He felt sick. Fear and dread washed over him. But then, almost without thinking, he was running again toward the scene. This couldn't happen. He couldn't let it happen. He reached up, flung off his backpack, and ran faster than he had ever run in his life. His legs felt strong and he lengthened his stride. He'd heard his mom say that's what you do in races. That's what you do when you have to win.

He was nearly upon them and Gregory heard himself shouting, "No! NO!!"

The dog paused in his chase and turned toward Gregory, suddenly standing quite still. Gregory stopped, too. The dog's long pink tongue lolled out of his mouth and his chest heaved.

"NO." Gregory was panting almost as hard as the dog. Sweat dribbled down his forehead and into his eyes, but he didn't dare move. They stood there, boy and dog, facing each other, a stand-off that dragged on as the seconds ticked past.

Then, with his heart pounding and hands trembling, Gregory took a step forward. It was an aggressive move, he knew it, aggressive and possibly provocative, but he had no choice. From the corner of his eye, he saw Teisha drag Tamara to her feet and, together, they ran down the road and up the steps to their front door. Tamara was crying, but Gregory blocked it out. He was looking straight into the tawny face of the giant dog.

"NO!" he shouted as loud as he could this time, and took another step forward. The dog faltered, suddenly seemed unsure of himself. With a flash of insight, Gregory recognized the fear in the dog's eyes, in his whole demeanor. But then it was gone and they stood there, staring at each other, neither moving, two statues in the middle of the road.

From somewhere behind, Gregory heard the sound of a car slowing on Clarke Street, turning in at the townhouse pillars. Help was on the way! Someone would leap out of that car, deal with the giant dog, and Gregory would be safe.

But the car didn't stop. It curved out and around the two of them and continued on its way. Gregory felt a spurt of intense anger. His father had always had great faith in people and their "underlying goodness," but at that moment, Gregory felt that his father had been wrong.

It was a big silver car, Gregory saw as it pulled away, crossing his line of vision. A big, shiny silver car and the driver sat high, a tall man, his bright red hair almost brushing the roof. The car moved on down the street, turned the corner, and disappeared.

The dog lowered his head and took a small step forward. That step in Gregory's direction made his heart jerk. He had to do something, and do it now.

"NO!" shouted Gregory. This time, he waved his arms and walked steadily forward toward the dog. Authority was in his voice and his actions.

It worked. The dog hesitated, took a step backward, then wheeled around and ran off at a scared gallop. He crossed the driveways that lined the other side of the street and vanished into the parkland that bordered Sprucewood Lane.

Shaking with relief and the effects of his frantic run, Gregory walked past the place where the dog had stood and up the steps to Teisha and Tamara's house. Before he had even knocked, the door flew open. Teisha grabbed him by the arm and dragged him in, slamming the door behind him.

"Is he gone?" she asked, her eyes wide.

"Yes. He disappeared into the park. I think he's gone down through the woods."

"Oh, Gregory, thank you."

"It's okay, Teisha," he said, wiping sweat from his forehead and trying not to think about how really scared he'd been.

NINE

The Nurse

Teisha led Gregory through their front hallway and into a kitchen that was exactly the same as his, except the colors and furniture were different. He sat and watched as she washed off Tamara's scraped hands and knees. Then she reached into a cupboard under the sink and pulled out a white Medicine Kit.

Tamara seemed pleased to be the center of her big sister's attention. "I am an accident victim, aren't I, Teisha?" she said. "That's what mommy says whenever we get a boo-boo ouchie, doesn't she, Teisha?"

"True," said Teisha. "You are a very brave accident

victim. Now come and sit down so I can get this bandaging on right."

"And that was a humongously big bad dog, wasn't it?"

"Yes," said Teisha, "he was really big and really bad."

But, despite his own fears, Gregory had been re-playing the incident in his mind. There'd been an uncertain, frightened look on the dog's face when he'd yelled at him. He seemed to shrink in on himself just before he ran away with his tail between his legs.

"I don't know," said Gregory. "I'm wondering if he was more scared than bad. You should have seen him run when I yelled at him. He looked terrified."

"Oh," said Tamara, "I don't care. I don't like him and I hope he keeps away from here."

"Maybe he's not used to being out loose and he's lost and scared," said Gregory. "Or, I don't know, maybe he thought you were playing."

"Then why was he chasing us?" said Teisha.

"Maybe an instinct?" said Gregory. "You know how dogs chase a ball or a Frisbee? I think some dogs just naturally like to chase things that are running, and he saw you running. Maybe it's a habit he's got."

"Well, it's a bad habit," said Teisha with a scowl.

"Yes, a very, very bad, bad, bad, bad, bad habit,"

said Tamara with a scowl and tone of voice that were identical to her sister's. Gregory and Teisha looked at each other and suddenly laughed.

"What are you laughing at?" said Tamara.

"You," said Teisha. "Now sit still, wiggle worm, or I'll never get you bandaged."

Teisha didn't use a little stick-on band-aid for each knee, which to Gregory's mind would have been sufficient. Instead, she folded up two thick cotton pads on which she squeezed a large dab of anti-bacterial cream. She placed these on Tamara's knees, then wrapped a long strip of gauze clear around each of her legs several times. "Not too tight and not too loose," she said. The last bit of each gauze strip she ripped lengthwise and tied the ends in a neat, flat knot.

"I learned this from my mom," said Teisha, bragging a little, but Gregory didn't mind. He was enjoying watching her hands as she worked. They were such small, pretty hands, but they looked strong, too. None of that stupid nail polish or long fake nails that some of the girls in his class were wearing. How they ever did anything with nails like that, he couldn't figure.

"Cool," he said when the last knot was tied. He was half-wishing he had some injury she could bandage up, too, but no such luck.

"She's a surgical nurse. Did you know that?" continued Teisha, turning to smile at him. Her eyes sure did sparkle when she smiled.

"Did you know that, Gregory?" she repeated.

"Oh ... no," answered Gregory. "I didn't know that. I mean, yes, I knew she was a nurse, but I didn't know she was that, what you said." How did she always manage to make him feel so flustered? What was the matter with him?

"She assists the surgeons. They can't do any operations without a surgical nurse. She's doing cardiac stuff today, isn't she, Tamara?" Tamara nodded.

"Do you know what cardiac means?" said Teisha.

"No," confessed Gregory, but he thought it sounded vaguely awesome.

"It means anything to do with the heart," said Teisha. "Did you think about my favorite number yet?" she asked.

"Ummm, no," said Gregory. To him, 37.0 was an uninspiring, edgy number, a number he could never like.

"I didn't think so," said Teisha, turning to Tamara. "Let's look at those hands now," and she did the same dressing and bandaging with Tamara's hands as she had done with her knees. When she was finished,

Teisha settled her with a glass of milk and a miniature Kit Kat from the big box of 200 Halloween treats their mother had hidden on a top shelf.

"Mom always hides treats up there. You'd think she'd notice that we always find them, but I guess she forgets."

"So, why do you like 37.0?" said Gregory.

Teisha tore open Tamara's treats for her and a small box of Smarties for herself. She handed a Kit Kat to Gregory, who didn't really want it but took it anyway. He didn't like chocolate. Not chocolate bars, chocolate milk, chocolate candies, not even chocolate ice cream or chocolate cake. But he ate the Kit Kat.

"Can't you guess?" said Teisha.

"No," said Gregory. "It sort of sounds like a cool number, but I think it's awkward. I think it's unbalanced," he said, choosing his words carefully. When Teisha glared at him and snapped her mouth shut, he said, "Well, maybe it's just a little bit unbalanced."

"It's no more unbalanced than 7.5," said Teisha. "I think 7.5 is unbalanced."

"Oh," said Gregory, not understanding how he had somehow initiated an argument about numbers. He had never had an argument about numbers before.

"I like 9," interrupted Tamara.

"Oh, I do, too," said Gregory, telling the truth, but also wanting to appease Teisha. "Nine is such a weird number, don't you think?"

"I don't think it's weird," said Tamara. "I think it's nice. It's pretty. I like it."

"If she likes it, why do you have to call it 'weird'?" said Teisha.

"What I mean is, that it's weird but in a good way," said Gregory. Both girls stared at him, their lips set in identical firm lines. Caught in the fiery gaze of the sisters, he stammered, "What I mean is ... is ... is ... what I mean is, that 9 is an odd number, but when you see it drawn out in a picture, you know, when you draw 9 dots on a page, lined up in a 3 by 3 matrix, it's a perfect square. It doesn't look like an odd number at all. Not like 7, for instance. When you draw 7 dots on a page, it always looks unbalanced and flabby, like there's one dot left over and it doesn't know where to go. But 9 is perfect. And its square root is 3, itself an odd, unbalanced number." He finished in a downslide of misery. Neither girl looked happy, and his explanations seemed to have made matters worse.

"Then why do you like 7.5, if 7 is so unbalanced?" said Teisha.

Her question almost took his breath away. He'd never thought of that before. "7.5 is different from 7," he protested.

"If you say so." Teisha tossed her head. "I think we should change the subject. I think we should talk about sensible things."

"Numbers are sensible," said Gregory, with a spurt of irritation.

"I think we should talk about the Save Our School campaign."

It was only on his way home later that Gregory realized he still had no idea why Teisha thought 37.0 was such a great number.

TEN

A Knock at the Door

"I had a call at work today from Mr. Gladstone," said Gregory's mom. They had just sat down to supper. Before Gregory had a chance to ask what it was about, there was a loud knock at the front door.

"Who on earth can that be, right at dinner time?" said his mom.

"What did Mr. Gladstone want?"

"I'll tell you in a minute. Go answer the door, please."

"But what did he want?"

"... Gregory, the door ..."

Gregory grabbed Chirp from his shoulder and put

him back in his cage, then went to the door. Maybe it was Matt, come to help him with his science homework. Or maybe it was Teisha, come to tell him about 37.0. When he pulled the door open and saw who was standing there, his face fell.

It was a tall, red-haired man, the man who had driven right on by in his big silver car when Gregory thought he was about to get his arms and legs ripped off. Gregory felt his face go stiff, but the man just smiled back. In one of his big strong hands, he held Gregory's backpack. "Is this yours?"

Gregory reached out and took it.

"Well, I found it beside the road up near the gates. Sorry, I had to open it to find some identification and your address."

Finally, Gregory found his voice. "Why didn't you stop?" he said. "I was in trouble. I thought you would stop and help, but you drove right by."

"What?" said the man, looking truly bewildered.

"I thought that dog was going to bite me. Well, he wouldn't have done that, but I didn't know it then. I was really scared."

"Who is it, Gregory?" his mother called.

"I thought you were doing tricks," said the man. "It looked to me like you had your dog really well trained.

I had no idea you were in trouble. I'm sorry. Are you okay?"

"I'm fine," said Gregory, his anger melting away. "He's not my dog, and he's not mean, either." He felt a little embarrassed, like he was making a big deal out of something trivial. But he had been scared. Really scared.

"Gregory, who is it?" repeated his mom, and she came to join him at the door. "What's this about a dog? Is that your backpack?"

"It's okay, Mom."

"It's just a big misunderstanding, for which I apologize," said the man, and he turned to go.

"Wait a minute," said Gregory's mom. "I don't mean to be rude, but who are you and what's this about?"

"My name is Alex Mackenzie," said the man. "I work at the Fire Station up on Bayfield. I was here this afternoon to see one of the townhouses that's for sale. On my way home just now, I found this backpack by the side of the road. I thought it might belong to the young fellow I saw earlier today, practicing dog tricks on the street. Or I should say, what I thought were dog tricks."

"Dog tricks? Gregory?" His mom looked at him to explain.

"A dog that lives up the street got loose today after school," said Gregory. "He was chasing Teisha and Tamara, but I came along and told him to go away."

"And I drove by," said Mr. Mackenzie, "but didn't even think of stopping to help because I thought your son was doing obedience training or some kind of dog tricks. Anyway, he did just fine all by himself, and now I think I'd better go. Nice to meet you both and, once again, apologies, Gregory."

Mr. Mackenzie was down the steps and driving away before Gregory or his mom even had a chance to thank him.

Gregory closed the front door and leaned against it, the backpack dangling in his hand. Maybe his dad had been right about human nature, after all.

"Gregory, you were very brave to scare off that dog to help your friends. But what if it had attacked you?"

"He wouldn't have done that."

"How do you know?"

Gregory shrugged. "I just know."

"Where did the dog come from?" She was talking fast now, frustrated with him, he knew, looking him straight in the eye and beginning to puff up like an inflating balloon.

"What?"

"Where does the dog live?"

Gregory swallowed. If he told her it was the little house up on Simcoe Street, she'd ask him what he was doing over there when school was in the opposite direction.

"It's a red house ..." He tried not to let his voice shake. How had this happened? All these blocks between him and his mom.

"Somebody needs to tell those people to keep their dog under control ..."

"No, Mom. It's okay. He's not there anymore, anyway. I told you. He ran away."

Suddenly, it was over. His mom reached out and hugged him. "Oh, Gregory," she said, "I'm sorry for being upset. You're a smart boy and I know you wouldn't do anything foolish. I have to learn to trust you more, don't I?"

Gregory thought about all the secrets he'd kept from her, all the lies and half-truths he'd told her since his dad had died. He felt miserable.

"Don't look like that, Gregory," she said. "I know you've been through a tough time since Daddy died. We both have. But come, sit down. We've got a nice dinner here and we're going to enjoy it. Hand me your plate. I'll warm it up."

It wasn't until they were almost finished their meal that his mom again mentioned the phone call from Mr. Gladstone.

"What did he want? Am I going to fail?" said Gregory.

"No," she said, "you're not going to fail. But Mr. Gladstone is concerned. He said you're having trouble in most of your subjects. He's going to arrange some extra help for you." She reached across the table and squeezed his hand. "He also told me about your math," she said and smiled.

"What about my math?"

"Gregory, Mr. Gladstone thinks you've got a special gift in math. He thinks—and these are his exact words—'Mrs. Gray, I think we've got a math genius on our hands.'"

"What?"

"That's exactly what he said. 'I think we've got a math genius on our hands.' He said something about Math Olympics."

"I wonder what that is," said Gregory as he started in on his cherry pie.

After his mom had tucked him in bed that night, she stopped on her way out the door. "Gregory," she said, "I've been missing out on a lot of things lately and

I'm sorry. I love you and I want you to tell me about things. You should have told me about that dog. You should have told me you were having trouble with your schoolwork. I want to know about everything important in your life. Okay?"

"Okay, Mom."

"Promise?"

"Promise."

"Is there anything else I should know? Anything else worrying you?"

"No, Mom."

"All right," she said, "sweet dreams, honey," and turned off the light.

It was a long time before Gregory could get to sleep. Two lies in one conversation. He was getting good at this.

ELEVEN

Save Our School

t had rained all morning, but a watery sun finally peeked through at noon. Gregory and Matt were heading out to the playground. Teisha hurried down the hall toward them.

"Where are you going, Gregory? Aren't you coming to the campaign meeting?"

"No, ma'am!" Mrs. Checklee's voice boomed out. "He's coming with me today, AGAIN, aren't you, Gregory? Didn't forget your detention, did you? Come on. Don't look so disappointed. There will be other soccer games, but right now Room 7 and all its glory awaits you."

With Mrs. Checklee marking papers at her desk and six other students sitting looking bored, Gregory roughed out some sample pictures of what he thought would be good campaign posters. The trouble was, he never could draw. His attempt to draw the schoolhouse with "Save Me" written across the front of it looked like a box of cereal. He sighed and pushed it away.

He stared at the clock. Just another fourteen minutes and fourteen seconds and they would be released. Looking at the clock, he began to think about time. He thought how time is all around us, like air, and yet we can't see it, hear it, or feel it. The only way to experience time is to pass through it. And you can only go forward, never backwards or sideways.

What exactly is time? thought Gregory, and he felt that familiar, slightly dizzy feeling he always got when his brain suddenly went catapulting somewhere deep and new. Can we only measure it as we move through it, with seconds and minutes and days, or are there other ways to measure it, other parts of it we don't know about yet? Then a very strange thought occurred to him. Does time have speed? We move along in time, but is time itself moving along some other kind of track? If it is, how fast is it going? What would happen if it went faster? If it went slower?

Somehow he knew that all the answers linked up with mathematics. Mathematics was at the root of everything.

"Gregory ..." Mrs. Checklee was looking at him, a puzzled smile on her face. The room was empty except for the two of them.

"Yes, Mrs. Checklee?"

"You can go now, Gregory. The detention is over. Didn't you hear me? Go get your jacket on and run outside for some fresh air before the bell rings."

During the few minutes of hubbub as the class settled down after lunch recess, Teisha came over to Gregory's desk. Her face was glowing.

"You missed a really great meeting," she said. "We got thirty more signs painted. We're going to do 90 or even 100 more. The Grade 8's nailed on the stakes, and we put a whole bunch of them along the sidewalk right at the front of the school. Isn't that great?"

"But it's going to rain tonight, isn't it? Won't that ruin them? Didn't you say you were getting plastic signs printed? When will those be ready?"

"It might not rain," said Teisha. "The plastic ones are supposed to arrive tomorrow morning. Mr. Sylvester has the petition forms done, though, and they're perfect."

"Have you got a coverage chart?"

"A what?"

Mr. Gladstone was speaking. "Take your seats, please, class. We've got a lot to do this afternoon."

"A coverage chart. It's a list that shows which students are going to visit which houses. It's so people don't get multiple visits from kids bugging them."

"Come on Grade 6's. Get the lead out," said Mr. Gladstone. "Into your seats, please."

"A coverage chart! Brilliant," said Teisha. "You should tell Mr. Sylvester about it. In all the rush, nobody even thought about a coverage chart. Oh, by the way," she said, "I've got something planned for after school today."

"You do?" said Gregory. "What?"

She smiled. "You'll have to wait and see."

As she turned to go to her desk, her hair swung out behind her, all long and dark and shiny.

Just like in a TV ad, thought Gregory, and suddenly felt hot all over.

TWELVE

51 Sections of Sidewalk

Dozens of "Save Our School" signs bristled along the edge of the sidewalk and across the school lawn like spines on a porcupine. Teisha and Tamara burst through the front door and came running down the steps. Teisha carried a big piece of bright purple sidewalk chalk.

"Time to try out The Experiment," she said, out of breath and grinning.

"What experiment?" said Matt.

"For Gregory," she said, "to help him walk to the Jiffy Mart."

"What?" said Gregory.

"Tamara and I are going to write numbers on each section of sidewalk from 1 to 51 ... we already counted them," she said. "There are 51 sections of sidewalk between the front of the school and the front of the Jiffy Mart."

"I don't get it," said Matt.

"Neither do I," said Gregory.

"It's simple," said Teisha. "Each day you walk one additional sidewalk section toward the Jiffy Mart on the way home from school. That way, little by little, you get closer and closer to the Jiffy Mart, but it will happen so slowly, you'll hardly notice. And we'll help you. We'll be right here."

"That'll take ages," said Matt.

"It will take exactly 51 days," she said, "but it'll work. After going one section closer to the Jiffy Mart each day, Gregory, you can turn around and go home the long way if you want to. Every day, though, you'll be one big step closer to your goal. Get it?"

"I don't know." In theory, it sounded pretty good, but Gregory wasn't sure what it would be like to actually do it. Still, it was worth a try. "Sure, let's do it," he said with more confidence than he really felt.

"Great," said Teisha, and she wrote a big purple

"1" in the corner of the section of sidewalk they were standing on. With Tamara skipping along beside her, she took a step forward and wrote "2" on the next section. Then another step and she wrote "3."

As the boys stood watching the girls doing the numbering, Matt said, "Look," and pointed to an old lady crossing the street up near the Jiffy Mart. Every few steps, the old lady stopped, took something out of a bag, and laid it on the sidewalk.

"Who is that?" said Matt. "What's she doing?"

"That must be who's putting dead daisies on the sidewalk," said Gregory.

"The dead-daisy lady. What a kook."

The old lady finished crossing the intersection and stepped up onto the curb, right over the spot where the concrete was broken. Gregory's heart lurched. He watched as she entered the Jiffy Mart. In a rising panic, he switched his gaze to Teisha and Tamara, busily numbering the sidewalk sections. Tamara was singing, "Ring around the rosy, Pocket full of posy, Hush-a, Hush-a, We all fall down," over and over again. They were getting closer and closer to the Jiffy Mart. Gregory closed his eyes. He couldn't watch.

Beside him again, Teisha said, "Did you see that old

lady? I think she was ..." but Teisha didn't finish her sentence. "Gregory," she said, staring at him, "are you all right?"

"I can't do it," said Gregory.

"Yes, you can," said Teisha.

"No, I can't. I can't even look at the spot, let alone walk to it."

"Maybe it's just the 'seeing' part that's making it hard," said Matt. "Why don't we blindfold you, walk you up to where the accident happened, then take the blindfold off? We don't need any stupid chalk numbers."

Teisha gave him a dark look. Gregory felt too weak to argue, but Matt's idea did sound like it might be helpful.

"All right, then," huffed Teisha, shoving the chalk into her pocket. Have it your way, Matt. Tamara, give me your hair band."

"No."

"Give it to me."

"No. It's my favorite. You can't have it."

"It's not for keeps, Tamara. I just want to borrow it for Gregory. We need to blindfold him so he won't be scared."

Reluctantly, Tamara gave up her hair band and

Teisha tied it around Gregory's head, tightly covering his eyes.

Gregory knew it wasn't going to work. He felt imprisoned, suffocated, and with darkness all around and the sidewalk uneven beneath his feet, he couldn't do it. But with Teisha on one side and Matt on the other, they began propelling him up the sidewalk toward the Jiffy Mart. Tamara walked backwards in front of them, offering words of encouragement as though Gregory were a puppy out for the first time on a leash.

"Come on, Gregory," she said. "Good boy ..."

"Tamara, be quiet," said Teisha.

Before he had gone a half-dozen steps, Gregory reached up, tore off the blindfold, and walked shakily back toward the school and the long route home.

"Come back, Gregory," called Matt.

"Let's try it again," called Teisha. "We can get a better blindfold."

But Gregory kept walking. Nothing in this world would ever induce him to go to that place again. It was over.

Behind him, he heard Teisha yell at Matt. "Now you've spoiled it. The numbering would have worked."

"Shut up, Teisha," said Matt. "It was a stupid idea."

Tamara started to cry. "Don't you yell at my sister.

You shut up. You're stupid."

Then he heard Matt's voice again. "Hey, Gregory," he yelled, "what if you got on my bike behind me and I pedal us to the Jiffy Mart? I can go really fast ... you'll hardly even know we're there, and we'll go right on by."

"Without turning his head, Gregory yelled, "No!" He was angry now, mostly with himself, but angry, too, with Matt and Teisha. And now they were fighting and it was all his fault.

"Pleeeeeease," called Teisha, "come back, Gregory."

"Hey, come on, man," said Matt. "Don't give up so easily." What he said flipped Gregory straight from anger into red-hot fury. "Leave me alone, all of you! Just leave me alone!"

"All right," yelled Matt, "I will," and Gregory heard the pop of his bike tires as he sped away.

The last thing Gregory heard as he started home the long way 'round was Tamara. She was crying. "Why is Gregory so mad, Teisha? Did we do something wrong?"

THIRTEEN

Apology x 2

Gregory heard the front door slam. It was his mom, home from work. Five minutes later, she was gone for her run ... a short one tonight, she'd said. He heaved a sigh. Since arriving home from school, he hadn't been able to think of anything but Matt and Teisha. They'd tried to help him, and he'd been nothing but ungrateful. He had to do something. He picked up the phone and called Matt. Mr. Taylor answered. He had his audio system turned way up loud, and one of the babies was crying even louder. He, or she, must be really mad about something.

"I'm sorry, Gregory," he shouted. "Matthew's not

home right now. He should be back soon, though. He's gone to help his mother with the groceries. I'll ask him to call you when they get in ... sorry, gotta go."

Gregory had to call Information to get Teisha's phone number. She answered on the third ring. Almost before she'd said, "Hello," he apologized.

"That's okay, Gregory," said Teisha. "I think you were brave to at least try it. Maybe the chalk was a dumb idea. Maybe Matt was right, after all."

"It wasn't dumb," said Gregory. "It just didn't work, that's all." He was anxious to get off the subject of the Jiffy Mart. "I want to get helping with the campaign," he said. "I asked my mom again about the posters. She said she could do some large ones for us, but she needs some ideas about what we want."

"I think they should be really big," said Teisha, "something that people can see from a distance. I don't think it matters what she puts on them as long as 'Centennial Public School' and 'Save Our School' are there."

Later that night, when he still hadn't heard back from Matt, Gregory called again. "Matt, I'm sorry I was so mad at you today. You were just trying to help me, I know."

"Yah, I know," said Matt. "It's okay. So what are you going to do?"

"I don't think there's much I can do."

"There's got to be something. I mean, you can't spend the rest of your life avoiding the Jiffy Mart. Especially if the school closes and the new school bus stop ..."

"I know. I know," said Gregory.

After the supper dishes were done, Gregory went into the front room and plunked down in the big white bean-bag chair at the front window. It was his favorite place to think. Chirp had had his shoulder time with Gregory and was singing and chittering away up on the curtain rod. Usually Gregory would have been playing with him, letting him dangle from his fingers or climb up his chest inside his shirt with his sharp, itchy, funny little toenails. But not tonight. Matt's words kept ringing in his head. He had to do something.

"You look worried, Gregory," said his mom, sitting down on the sofa with the newspaper. "What's up?"

"I guess I'm thinking about the school closing and what we can do to stop it."

"Not an easy task," she said, "not when money

and politics are involved."

"Money?"

"Yes, money, and lots of it. The school board is spending hundreds of thousands of dollars building the new school and they want it to be a success when it opens in January. They understand the history angle of Centennial and are sympathetic, I'm sure, but little schools that serve only a few hundred students are probably just way too expensive to run. The heating costs alone must be horrendous."

Gregory was beginning to feel desperate. What was he going to do? This closure just could not happen, and here was his own mom siding with the enemy.

"Maybe they could raise our taxes?" he said.

"Ha! Ha!" she answered. "Not on your life."

"Well, maybe we just need more people to fight it. Maybe with more people, they would listen."

She looked over at him. "Why are you so invested in this? Why is this so important to you?"

Gregory felt his face flush. He knew the real reason, but it wasn't something he could explain to his mom. Not now. Not after all this time.

"I dunno," he said. "It's just ... it's just the only school I've ever been to and I like it ..." He was grasping for words and ideas now. "... I like it and ... and ... and ...

I'd hate for Mr. Gladstone to lose his job."

"Well, you know I'll do everything I can to help, including painting big posters, like I told you. You do need to give me some direction, though," she said, "you know, with colors and design and, of course, what message you want to convey."

Gregory told his mom what Teisha had said, then added, "And I've been thinking we should use the school colors on the posters, you know, purple and gold."

"I like it."

"Maybe you could have happy kid faces on the posters, too?"

"Yes, lots of happy kids, older and younger, running around the playground with all the big old maple trees lining the fences."

"Sounds good, Mom. I think we could put the posters up in central locations like the library, the community center, the big grocery store up on Yonge Street, and maybe one in the mall, too." He didn't mention the Jiffy Mart.

He told her then about the school's plan to get signs on people's lawns. He'd also been thinking about the petition Mr. Gladstone and Mr. Jacobson had told them about in the assembly. How could they get a lot of people to sign the petition? Door to door was fine, but surely there must be a more efficient way to do it. Just calculating the (Time + Effort) that would be required to gain only one door-to-door signature made it clear that it was a logically and mathematically unsound approach.

Then he noticed the Ad's section of his mom's newspaper that had slipped out and fallen onto the floor.

He leaned over and picked it up. "Do you think we could put an ad in the community paper to advertise the campaign and ask people to sign our petition?"

"Sure," said his mom. "It would cost something to do that, though."

"I know, but the School Council gave us money for signs. Maybe they would pay for advertising in the paper, too. We could tell people to come to the school to sign, or maybe we could have petitions in other places, like the library and the community center. Maybe we could have a petition for people to sign in every place where we put one of your posters. We could organize an online petition, too," he said. "Mr. Singh would help us with that, I know."

Gregory was getting excited. Maybe this was going to work, after all.

FOURTEEN

0, 1, 8, 11, 88, 101, ___

When Gregory woke up Friday morning, he already couldn't wait for Math Club. Despite all the upset and subsequent planning of the last few days, he hadn't forgotten about Teisha's number pattern. He couldn't wait to hear the solution.

"Teisha," said Mr. Singh, "you presented an extraordinarily difficult number pattern for the class on Tuesday. Has anyone solved it?" He wrote the pattern on the board: 0, 1, 8, 11, 88, 101, ___ , and looked around the room. "No? Well, neither have I. Teisha, the floor is yours."

Teisha went up to the board and wrote l l l in the blank. She turned to the group, a big expectant smile on her face, but there was no response, not even from Mr. Singh. Everyone looked as confused as ever.

"You'll have to explain it for us," said Mr. Singh.

"Don't you notice anything about these numbers?" she said. "Don't you see something funny about them?"

Gregory's heart sank. He'd been worried that Teisha was pulling a prank. What did she mean, "funny"? Numbers weren't funny.

"Don't you notice that they're all made up of zeros, ones and eights?" She looked at the class expectantly.

"Yes, we can see that," said Mr. Singh, "but I do not understand your sequence."

Gregory was thinking hard. What was it about these three digits that made them different from all others? He stared at the board and made his mind a blank. Then, in a flash of insight, he had it.

Each of the digits looked the same whether it was viewed forward or backward. Still, he did not understand the number pattern.

"These digits are all reversible," said Teisha. "Whether you read them in real life or in a mirror, they look the same." Again, she stared expectantly at the group, but still there was no sign of recognition of the solution.

She continued. "I decided to use numbers that had only these reversible digits in them, right?" There were tentative nods and murmurs of assent.

"Then why isn't the answer to the pattern 108, not 111?" asked Reggie. He always sat in the front seat at Math Club. "Those are all reversible digits."

"I know," said Teisha, "but I also wanted numbers that would read the same forwards and backwards, too, like 11 or 101. With 108, you couldn't read it backward and have it be the same. Backward it would be 801 not 108. So the next number in my sequence has to be 111. Either way you read it, it's 111."

Suddenly, there were laughs of recognition.

"Well done, Teisha," said Mr. Singh. "Excellent work. Impressive originality of thought. Congratulations and thank you for sharing it with us. Now, everybody," he said, "the end-of-lunch recess bell is going to ring any second and, before that happens, I'm going to tell you the problem we'll be discussing on Tuesday. I want you to think about it over the weekend. Here it is. Listen carefully. If a frog is ten meters from a wall, how many jumps will it take him to reach the wall if, each time he jumps, he goes exactly half the remaining distance? Got it?" And he repeated it once more, slowly and clearly, to make sure everyone had understood. "Good. See you Tuesday."

On the way to their lockers, Gregory congratulated Teisha. "That was a great number pattern, Teisha. It wasn't quantitative, like everybody was expecting. It was more visual. I guess you could say, artistic."

"Thanks," said Teisha. "I bet your mom would have solved it, her being an artist and all."

Gregory laughed. "I should have asked for her help, but she's terrible in math. What gave you the idea, anyway?"

"Oh, that was easy. I was in the Jiffy Mart a while ago and found myself reading MR. YAMAMOTO's name on the window from the inside. It's all in capitals and I noticed that all the letters, except the 's' looked the same whether you read them from inside or outside the store. The name 'YAMAMOTO' was backwards, but the letters weren't. I thought that was pretty cool. It gave me the idea to use reversible digits, and then I decided to use numbers that read the same forwards and backwards, too."

"Awesome," said Gregory.

"Thanks," said Teisha. "Meet you at the pillars after school?"

Gregory looked at her.

"To start our campaign visits?"

"Oh, right," said Gregory, and tried to pretend he'd remembered.

FIFTEEN

Campaign Duty

After school, Teisha, Matt, and Gregory started visiting houses. A coverage chart had been developed by the school office, as Gregory had suggested. The three of them were assigned Simcoe Street and Sprucewood Lane. Teisha's mom loaned them their bundle buggy to carry the signs. They took turns pushing it up the street. Matt had a clipboard from the school, with three pages of blank petition sheets and a black ink pen attached with a long string.

On one side of Simcoe alone, they visited twenty-two houses and, where the people were at home, they got fifteen signatures and put up six signs.

"Why do people sign the petition but not want to put a sign on their lawn?" complained Teisha, hammering one into the ground. "It doesn't make any sense."

They started down the other side of Simcoe Street. Seventeen houses, twelve signatures, and seven signs later, they approached the little red house where the big tawny-colored dog lived. The fence over in the corner was still trampled down and there was no sign of the dog anywhere. They unlatched the gate and walked up the narrow pathway to the front door.

It was Teisha's turn to knock. No answer. They counted to ten (instructions from Mrs. Checklee), then knocked again, louder. If there was no answer after the third knock, they would leave. Teisha was just raising her knuckles the third time when the door was jerked open. It was the red-dress girl, the girl Gregory and Teisha had seen sitting and smoking on the dead-tree bench earlier in the week. She wasn't wearing a red dress now, though. She had on baggy jeans and an old green plaid shirt. Her face was blotchy and her eyes were red and swollen. Gregory recognized the signs of an all-day cry.

"What do you want?" she demanded.

"We're students from Centennial Public School," said Matt. It was his turn to talk. He glanced down at the speech card in his hand. "The School Board is planning to close our school in January and send us to a new school. We're asking the community to support us in our fight to save our school. We hope you will sign our petition to keep Centennial open and allow us to put a 'Save Our School' sign on your lawn." He held out the clipboard but the girl was already closing the door.

"Get lost," she said. "I couldn't care less about the stupid school."

"Well, we do," said Teisha, pushing back on the door. "Maybe your mom should come and sign the petition for us if you're not going to."

"My mom isn't home and, even if she was, I wouldn't bother her with your problems," said the girl. "We've got enough of our own," and she slammed the door shut.

"You mean, like your dog being lost?" shouted Gregory. The instant the words were out of his mouth, he regretted it. He had a sudden vision of the girl yanking open the door and pounding him a good one.

"Shut up," she yelled.

"You need to put up posters with the dog's picture and name on it," shouted Teisha. "What's his name, anyway ... or is he a girl?"

"HIS name is Mickey," came the muffled reply, "and why don't you mind your own business?"

"We're just trying to help," yelled Teisha. "It says on the Internet that if your pet is lost, you should put up posters with a picture of him, and your phone number, and offer a reward. You should call the local Humane Society, too, to see if anyone has found him and brought him in."

The door opened.

"What's their number?" said the girl.

"I don't know," said Teisha, "you'd have to Google it."

"I haven't got a computer," she said. "Not everybody in the world has a computer, you know."

"Here," said Matt, extending the clipboard, "write your phone number up here in the corner and I'll look it up and call you."

"Thanks," said the girl. She wrote down her number and started to shut the door again, gently this time.

"Well, you could at least sign our petition," said Teisha.

"Oh, yah," said the girl, and wrote "Sam Biggs" on the sheet in big scrawling letters.

"Sam?" said Teisha doubtfully, reading the signature upside down. "You don't look like a Sam to me."

"Samantha," said the girl, her face set in a hard line

as she stared at Teisha. "My name is Samantha, okay, but people call me Sam."

"Can we put a sign on your lawn, Sam?" said Matt.

"No," she said, "I don't think my mom would like that."

No one was home at the next two houses and, at the third house, the people didn't speak English. The fourth house signed the petition and let them put a sign on the lawn. It was late by the time they got back to Clarke Street. The sun would soon set. They only needed a few minutes to do Sprucewood Lane, they told each other, because there weren't many houses down there.

It was dark and very quiet under the spruces. The only sound was the harsh crunching of the gravel under their feet.

"I say we skip any house where there's no lights on," said Matt.

Gregory and Teisha agreed. It was the first time the three of them had agreed on something without an argument.

Four little cabins, sitting close together as though for company, lined the street to the left. All in darkness. They passed them by, walking fast. Then there was a ramshackle house. The windows were broken and the front door hung loose. A sudden gust of wind caught it and it squealed on rusty hinges. The three of them jumped.

"Oh," said Teisha, "I think we should go home now. There's only one more house down at the end and it's all dark."

"Yah, let's go," said Matt. "Nobody's home ..."

Lights suddenly flared in the two front windows.

They stopped dead in their tracks.

"Someone is home," whispered Gregory.

"Yes," said Teisha. "Someone I don't want to meet. Let's get out of here."

Just then, a loud bark came from inside the house. They looked at each other.

"It's the dog," said Gregory, "the dog that belongs to that girl, Sam. I'd know that bark anywhere. Come on, we've got to find out why whoever lives here has got her dog."

Before they had even climbed the wooden steps, the door of the house was flung open and a rectangle of yellow light spilled out over them. An old lady stood in the doorway.

"Hush, Puppy," she called over her shoulder, "we've got company." She turned to her visitors. "Come in, you three. You look like you've seen a ghost. Come in. COME IN!"

Something about her commanding tone and manner made them obey. They stumbled into the room. The dog continued to bark from behind a closed door. The old lady ignored the racket and stared down at them through hugely magnified glasses. Behind the thick lenses, her eyes loomed strange and sinister. Her hands, hoisted on her hips, looked very strong.

He had seen her before; Gregory knew it. But who was she? And what were they doing, going into her house? Hadn't Mrs. Checklee made it clear that under no circumstances were students to enter any house they visited?

A pitcher of daisies sitting on a low table was the clue Gregory needed. It was the dead-daisy lady ... the crazy dead-daisy lady.

"Well," said the old lady, "who are you and what do you want? Quiet, Puppy," she ordered, and the dog was suddenly silent.

"I'm Teisha," said Teisha, a little tremor in her voice. "This is Gregory and that's Matt. We're students from Centennial Public School. The School Board is planning to close ..."

"Is that your dog in there?" interrupted Gregory. His

fearfulness and the strangeness of the situation made him forget all about being polite. "Or ...?"

He was cut off by a loud crash.

"Puppy, you naughty Puppy! I already gave you a treat." The old lady hurried across the room and pulled open the door.

It was Sam's dog, all right, but he was all shiny and looked like he'd just been bathed and brushed. He was standing with both front feet up on the kitchen counter. A green plastic bowl was still spinning on the floor and the contents of what looked like a whole bag of cookies was scattered everywhere.

"Oh, you bad Puppy," said the old lady, bending to pick up the bowl. "You bad, bad Puppy." But she was laughing, and the dog didn't look the least bit intimidated. He just kept running around, grabbing cookies and swallowing them whole before the old lady could get to them. Finally, she gave up and let him have the last few. She was laughing and wiping her eyes. "Oh, I guess boys will be boys," she said and put the bowl back up on the counter. When she laughed, her whole face changed. She looked nice now, friendly, even.

With the cookies all gone, the dog turned his attention to the newcomers. He trotted toward them and barked. It was so loud in the small room that the china plates hanging on the wall rattled. Teisha caught her breath.

"Don't be afraid," said the old lady. "He's friendly. Lots of bark in him, but no bite," and she reached down and took hold of his collar. "He came to my door two days ago," she said. "He was soaked and muddy, half-drowned in the creek that runs behind this place. He was hungry, too, though I can't say he looks underfed." She laughed again, and scratched his ears. "There's no identification on his collar," she said, "but I call him Puppy. Not because he's small, but because he's so sweet. Let him get to know you," she said, "and you'll see. This boy has a kind heart. There you go, Puppy. Go welcome our visitors, there's a boy."

The dog trotted toward them. "Oh, oh, oh," cried Teisha.

"It's okay," said Gregory. "She's right. He's friendly. See?" He held out his hand. Even though he now knew the old lady wasn't crazy, and the dog wasn't crazy either, he couldn't help feeling a little shiver of fear as the dog came toward him.

The cold wet nose touched his hand. Then there was the sudden warmth of a lick. Then another and another.

"Look," said Teisha. "He's giving you kisses."

"Of course, he's giving kisses," said the old lady. "He's friendly. Didn't I say?"

Then Gregory told her how the dog scared people who passed his house, barking and running after them. He told her about the broken fence and how he had chased and frightened Teisha and Tamara.

"He's just like people," said the old lady. "When he's frightened, he pretends to be brave but, inside, he's scared to death. But you're right, he is nervous. I guess people running upsets him, and dogs as well as people do funny things when they're upset."

"We know who he belongs to," said Matt. "A girl who lives up on Simcoe Street. I think we should call her. She's been really upset since Mickey ran away."

"Mickey!" exclaimed the old lady. "What a terrible name for a dog. But go ahead and phone this girl. I can't have that on my conscience. She'd better treat him right, is all I can say."

SIXTEEN

Sunshine Marshall

Matt phoned Sam. "She's on her way," he said. "She'll be here in a few minutes."

The old lady went and sat down on the sofa. The dog followed her and put his big lion head in her lap. Gregory, Matt, and Teisha were still standing awkwardly inside the front door.

"Don't be standing there like three dumb monkeys," said the old lady. "Come in and sit down, for goodness sake. I guess since you've told me who you are, I'd better introduce myself. My name is Sunny Marshall. Miss Sunny Marshall," and she scratched behind the dog's ears. "My nephew told me this would happen," she said. "He said I shouldn't get too attached, that someone obviously loves this dog and that I couldn't keep him. He told me I should call the Humane Society to report I'd found him … or rather, that he'd found me. He said someone would be looking for him. I guess Alex was right."

Since recognizing who she was, Gregory had been bursting to ask his question. "We've seen you on Clarke Street, haven't we? You leave a trail of daisies on the sidewalk."

"Yes," she answered, glancing up at Gregory. "You noticed them?"

He nodded.

"Crazy old lady, right?"

"No," said Gregory, but felt ashamed because that was exactly what he'd thought.

"I'll tell you something," she said. "When you get old, and your eyesight isn't what it used to be, and your memory starts playing tricks on you, well, then you might start doing some crazy-looking things yourself. One day, not too long ago, I went up to the Jiffy Mart for a few things and, on the way home, I got all turned around. I couldn't figure out which direction home was. I had to go to someone's door and ask them. Can you imagine how humiliating that was? Well, since then, I decided to leave a trail so it would never happen again.

"That's when I started gathering the daisies," she said. "There's enough of them on my lawn and in the field behind me. I leave a daisy on the sidewalk every few steps, then on my way back home from the Jiffy Mart, I follow them. I need to put down new ones every trip I make because the daisies disappear. Wind blows them away, I guess, or people pick them up. Do you take them?" She gave the three of them a sharp look.

"No," said Gregory.

"Well, a daisy trail is a poor solution to my problem, anyway," said Miss Marshall. "I was hoping I could train Puppy to walk me up to the Jiffy Mart and home again. But Alex, my nephew ... do you know Alex? He's a fireman up at the station on Bayfield Avenue?"

"He's your nephew?" said Gregory. "Mr. Mackenzie?"

"Yes. Do you know him?"

"Not really. I just met him once."

"Well," said Miss Marshall, "he says that dogs need to be specially trained for that kind of work, and I guess he's right." She leaned over and kissed the bridge of Mickey's big pointy nose, then looked up at them.

"What did you come to my door for, anyway? It wasn't to discuss dogs, now, was it?"

"No," said Teisha, and started over with the Save Our School speech.

"Why don't you want a new school?" said Miss Marshall.

"It was built in 1967, the 100th anniversary of Confederation. It's part of our history," Teisha said. "It's important to the community, too, with all kinds of activities taking place there after school, like Scouts and Girl Guides and yoga classes."

"Well, then, I guess I can see your point," said Miss Marshall. "Put up a sign on my lawn if you want to, though not many folks will see it, and, here, give me your petition."

Matt handed her the clipboard and she signed it.

"Are you going to write an article about your plight for the *Markham Herald*?" she said, but was interrupted by loud banging and yelling at the door.

"Mickey! Mickey!"

The big dog bounded to the door and started barking, his bushy tail wagging furiously, his whole body almost turning inside out with excitement. Sam didn't wait to be let in. She burst into the room and was down on her knees, hugging Mickey before any of the others even had a chance to blink.

"Oh, Mickey, Mickey, Mickey."

Gregory felt a lump form in his own throat as he remembered almost losing Chirp.

In her rush, Sam had neglected to bring a leash. Miss Marshall loaned her the tie from her dressing gown. "You get some ID for that dog collar," she said, "or, better still, get your vet to put in an identification chip. You bring this tie back, too, you hear? I need it."

Sam agreed to return it the following day, Saturday.

"Call me before you come," said Miss Marshall, "so I know when to expect you. Here's my phone number. My nephew tells me not to open the door to strangers, and I guess he's right, though I opened it to you lot tonight, didn't I, and I'm glad I did. I will miss Puppy, though, that's for sure," and she leaned over and patted the big head. "But I'm happy to see you happy, young lady, and there's no doubt this dog loves you to pieces. Bring him with you, will you, when you return my dressing gown tie? Here, you'd better give me your number, too, so I know where Puppy is ... I mean Mickey ... just in case you forget."

"I won't forget," said Sam, tying the makeshift leash to Mickey's collar.

"Miss Marshall gasped. "I've just thought of something. Would you be interested in earning some pocket money?"

"Maybe," said Sam a little warily.

"Well, I wouldn't mind some help two or three times a week going up to the Jiffy Mart, and, by my reckoning, you and Mickey might be just the ticket."

"You mean it?" said Sam.

"Of course, I mean it. I wouldn't have said it if I didn't mean it," said Miss Marshall. "We could start tomorrow, try it for a week, and see how it goes. What do you say?"

Gregory looked at Sam's beaming face and wondered how he could ever have been afraid of her. Then he looked over at Miss Marshall. She was still pretty strange with her thick glasses and big bony hands, but crazy? No way. And Mickey? Well, he was just one big softie.

SEVENTEEN

The Solution

That night, Gregory and his mom hurried through a supper of leftovers. She was skipping her run tonight. The Campaign Meeting started at 7 PM. They'd barely get there on time as it was.

All the parents were expected to attend, but Teisha's mom had to work and Matt's parents were too busy with the babies. It was up to Gregory to "take notes," Teisha said.

"So, she's 'the boss,' is that it?" His mom gave him a mischievous smile.

"She thinks she is," said Gregory and held out a little piece of lettuce to Chirp, who'd been having shoulder time, all the while squawking for treats. He'd already had a crumb of bread, a piece of raw carrot, and part of a green bean.

"That's it," said Gregory. "No more."

Gregory's mom parked the car on the street and, together, they hurried up the main front steps and into the school. Luckily, it was still raining heavily. Gregory had had a few anxious moments earlier, when his mom had said they'd walk up to the school, but the rain had come to his rescue.

Most of the handmade campaign signs lining the walkway had been reduced to soggy, unreadable messes. The plastic signs, though, looked great, except for the misspelling that read "Centennail" on all one hundred of them.

"At least we got them for free," said Gregory, "but Teisha was really upset."

Gregory and his mom walked through the muted lighting of the near-empty school hallways. It looked and felt so alien without the usual hubbub and noise. They passed Mr. Singh's darkened classroom. It made Gregory think again about the jumping frog problem. Down at the end of the hall, they saw a cluster of parents and some students, all gathered at the open gym doors. As they got closer, they could see people lining up to sign petition sheets that were taped on the wall.

Gregory looked around. It was the most crowded he'd ever seen the gym. People were talking loudly, and a lot of them were milling around the coffee table at the back. Then he saw Mr. Mackenzie. He would have been hard to miss, standing a head taller than anyone else and his red hair blazing like a forest fire under the fluorescent lights.

"Look, Mom. It's Mr. Mackenzie. Did you know he's Miss Marshall's nephew?"

"Yes, you told me."

"He doesn't look at all like Miss Marshall, though, does he?" said Gregory, but his mom wasn't listening. She was busy pushing forward in the petition-signing line. Gregory looked again for Mr. Mackenzie but he had disappeared. Probably sat down, thought Gregory. It was hard to imagine that he and Miss Marshall were related. Still, she was pretty tall. Maybe Miss Marshall used to have red hair like that, too, before it turned all white. She must have a sister if Mr. Mackenzie was her nephew. Or maybe she had a brother. Gregory was thinking about that when his mother tapped him on the shoulder.

"I've signed," she said. "Now it's your turn," and she handed him the pen.

"I don't think kids are allowed," he said.

"I don't know why not. You're the ones most going to be affected and, Gregory, you know what you're doing and what the issues are. Go ahead and sign."

So he did, in his best grown-up writing.

All through the meeting, Gregory did his best to pay attention, but he couldn't focus. His thoughts kept bouncing back and forth between the Save Our School campaign and the jumping frog problem ... purple and gold borders on the posters ... frogs are green ... hop, hop, hop, hop, halfway each hop ... is that possible? Is it possible to save the school? I can't go to the new bus stop ... but the frog would go anywhere ... he would hop toward Mr. Singh's wall; he would hop toward the spot ... but he's bigger than the space left to jump ... how could he do it? How can we save the school? ...

"Gregory. We're going now."

He looked up. The meeting was over.

On their way out to the parking lot, Mr. Mackenzie caught up with them.

"Rain's stopped," he said.

"Yes," his mom replied, pushing Gregory ahead of her toward their car.

"Good meeting," said Mr. Mackenzie.

"Yes, it was."

"Well, I hope we win this battle," said Mr. Mackenzie and smiled down at Gregory, "for all our sakes."

"I do, too," said Gregory, "I really do, and it is like a battle, isn't it?"

"Yep. Certainly is. Anything I can do to help, you just let me know, Gregory ... Mrs. Gray. Well, good night to you both," and he strode off, whistling.

"Don't encourage him, Gregory," said his mom when they got into the car.

"What do you mean?"

"Nothing. Just don't encourage him, okay?"

That night, Gregory had a hard time getting to sleep. Though he'd tried desperately to avoid thinking about the real possibility that the school might close, it kept circling around and around his head like a mosquito on a hot summer night. If worse came to worst and it really happened, and the school bus stop was outside the Jiffy Mart, what could he do? What would he do?

Maybe he could get his mom to move. No. She'd never do that, not without a good reason, and the moving costs would be too much. Not a good solution.

He'd already investigated the possibility of getting on the bus at another stop, and had to abandon it. It was all in the letter that had been sent home to parents. There were only going to be three bus stops, one in front of the Jiffy Mart, and one near each of the other schools that was closing, and they were away across town.

Gregory had even Googled legal issues about school bus stops, but there was nothing helpful there. It just had some safety rules about the ten-foot "danger zone" around stopped school buses, and how kids should make sure the driver could see them. How, if they dropped something in the danger zone, they should never stop to pick it up. Stuff like that. Nothing about bus stops, except that these were "solely determined by the School Board and at the School Board's discretion."

Finally, in frustration, Gregory abandoned the bus-stop line of thinking. It was making him dizzy and a bit panicky. He tried to settle his mind on the jumping frog problem. It was mathematically impossible. Wasn't it?

In a tangle of sheets, he finally fell asleep, only to awaken a short while later with his heart pounding.

He had the solution, not just to the jumping frog

problem, but the solution to his far more important problem, as well.

He knew what he was going to do. What he HAD to do. He'd been living in fear for so long, it was wrecking his life. Ever since the accident, he'd been running away from all the things that frightened him. He'd been afraid of being at the broken concrete curb where his dad had died, afraid even of looking at the spot. Afraid of the Jiffy Mart and that whole corner. Afraid of the bike he used to love. Afraid of the school closing. Afraid of the new school bus stop. He'd even been afraid of poor scared Mickey. It had to stop.

"No more running scared," he whispered into the darkness. But even as his lips formed the words, the boldness of the moment melted away, leaving behind only the cold chill of fear.

EIGHTEEN

The Jumping Frog

Next morning, before the sun was even up, Gregory forced himself out of bed. It was now or never. As quickly and as quietly as he could, he got dressed and crept down the stairs. He was shivering, whether from cold or fear, he didn't know, but now that he'd decided what to do, he felt a strange sense of urgency. He had to do this, and he had to do it quickly, before he changed his mind.

When he reached the bottom of the stairs, he heard Chirp stirring in his cage. A flood of warmth filled Gregory's heart. How he loved Chirp. But he pushed the thought aside as he hunched into his jacket, eased open the front door, and slipped outside.

It was cold. He could see his breath. The sky was a milky gray and the world around him was devoid of color, flat and lifeless. The street was empty. It had rained again through the night. Water dripped from the trees. A lot more leaves had come down; the lawns and sidewalks were littered with them.

Gregory walked out through the crooked pillars and turned left, toward the Jiffy Mart. His heart pounded and his legs felt weak.

Theoretically, he told himself, just like the frog going halfway and then halfway again, I will never get there. I will never have to stand on the spot where my dad died, so it's okay to go there.

Even as he reassured himself, he felt the hollowness of the words echoing back to him. But he kept on. Slowly but resolutely, Gregory walked up the sidewalk toward the Jiffy Mart. On and on, each step an increasing torture.

Surely he must be halfway there by now. He glanced up, tried not to look at the spot, just at the Jiffy Mart, and, yes, he was almost halfway.

Despite the cold, he was boiling hot now. His shirt under his jacket was wet with sweat. He kept his eyes down, watching his runners carry him forward. His knees had started to tremble, but he ignored it. Instead, he focused on a knot in his runner lace. Why hadn't he fixed that? It had bothered him for weeks. He saw a few faded daisies in the grass beside the sidewalk. Miss Marshall had put them there just a few days ago when this thing he was doing now, this walking to the Jiffy Mart, had seemed impossible.

Yes, impossible. Impossible. IMPOSSIBLE, the silence around him seemed to shout. It IS impossible. I CAN'T DO THIS ... I CAN'T DO THIS ... I CAN'T ...

Gregory's heart pounded in his ears. His breath came hard and sharp. His legs were rubber and his shirt lay cold and clammy, like some dead thing, against his skin. For a brief moment, he hesitated. In his mind, he saw himself whirling around and running home. But then, with a little sob, he moved forward. I HAVE to do this. I HAVE TO.

He turned his thoughts to the frog, the mathematically impossible journey of the frog. Theoretically, he told himself again, just like the frog, I will never stand on the spot where dad died, so it's okay. The frog. THE FROG. And this time, Gregory FELT the frog. He didn't just think about the frog. HE WAS THE FROG. Halfway, then halfway again, and then halfway again ... again and again to infinity ...

I CAN DO THIS. He ground it out between clenched teeth. I AM THE FROG. I AM THE FROG.

And against all impossible odds, Gregory started a slow jog toward the Jiffy Mart and the spot that had haunted him for so long.

I CAN DO THIS. I CAN DO THIS. I CAN DO THIS. It was a mantra, beat out in the steady rhythm as his feet hit the pavement.

Closer he got, and closer. Then, miraculously, he was crossing the intersection, headed straight for the Jiffy Mart. There were no cars. No people. Just him and his runners and his rubber legs moving forward. And then, the spot, that gouge in the concrete curbing smashed out by their car that night so long ago ... the spot ... it was right there in front of him.

Gregory stood still. He looked at that horrible gouge. It wasn't as big as he'd thought. Now that he was up close, it even looked ordinary, somehow. Nobody would ever know, just by looking at it, what had happened here. Nobody would ever know how this broken piece of concrete had come to represent everything Gregory had been running away from since that night.

He was breathing hard and his heart was pounding. "Theoretically, I will never stand on the spot," he said, and then took a big step forward. "But I am standing here," he said. "This is where it happened."

He felt himself trembling. He looked around and remembered the screeching slam as the truck broadsided them and tossed them like a toy across the intersection. He remembered the bang and flash and burning smell of the airbags. He remembered the broken glass, falling like rain inside the car. He remembered his dad's face. And then his stillness. The silence. The cold.

Gregory looked around and remembered it all with perfect clarity. But there was no smashed windshield now, no swirling snowflakes, no bright lights, just ordinary gray, rain-soaked pavement all around.

Gregory turned and looked in through the windows of the Jiffy Mart. It was dark in there. Not open yet. Taped on the inside of the front door was one of his mother's posters for the Save Our School campaign.

Gradually, the shaking stopped. Gregory's heart stilled. The sun rose and sent bright fingers across the blue, now cloudless sky. The whole world sparkled after the rain. Despite the cold, Gregory felt a sense of comfort, like a warm blanket, wrap itself around him. Suddenly, it was as if he were sharing this moment with his father and his mother, that they were both somehow there with him.

"It's all right, Gregory," he seemed to hear his father's voice. "Everything is going to be all right."

Gregory threw up his arms then like a prizefighter after a win, and danced, jumping up and down. "Yes," he shouted, "everything is going to be all right!"

He turned then and, with a heart lighter than he could ever remember, he ran back across the intersection and down Clarke Street, toward home. He was running faster now and laughing. He laughed at himself. He laughed at the puddles blazing in the sun. He laughed at the whole big, wonderful world. He ran in through the crooked pillars and on up the roadway. He ran with all his strength in long winner strides, and this time he wasn't running scared.

NINETEEN

No More Secrets, No More Lies

Gregory's mother met him at the front door. She had her dressing gown on any-which-way and her hair was standing practically straight up.

"Gregory, where have you been?" She pulled him close and hugged him hard. "I got up and found your bed empty and then the front door unlocked. I've been almost out of my mind. I was just about to call the police."

"It's okay, Mom," said Gregory.

"It's not okay. Where have you been?"

Gregory grinned at her and took off his jacket. Now

that he'd stopped running, he was cold. Freezing cold. He began to shiver.

"Look at you. You're soaking wet. Your hair, too. Where have you been? What's going on?"

"I've been up to the Jiffy Mart, Mom." His teeth started to chatter and he wrapped his arms around himself, but the smile on his face grew even bigger.

"The Jiffy Mart? Why on earth were you up at the Jiffy Mart at this hour? What are you smiling about? You look like you've just won a marathon."

"I think I have," said Gregory with a laugh. He was shivering now in earnest.

"You go on upstairs and into a hot shower this minute. Get on some warm clothes and come back down to breakfast. And then, young man, we're going to talk. I want to know why you were running a marathon up to the Jiffy Mart, and why you're smiling at me like a giant Cheshire cat. Go on. Get a move on." Gregory could tell she was trying to sound fierce, but the brand new grin on her own face wouldn't let her.

Later, over hot chocolate and toasted English muffins, dripping with butter and heaped high with cream cheese and bright red strawberry jam, Gregory told his mom everything. At last, there were no more secrets. No more lies.

Gregory had finished emptying the dishwasher and was cleaning out Chirp's cage, when he heard his mom thumping around down in the basement.

"Gregory, can you come help me, please?" she called.

He found her halfway up the cellar steps, carrying the framed "In Everything Give Thanks" poster.

"This is heavy. Give me a hand, will you?"

Together, they lugged it upstairs. Gregory's mom got out the Windex and paper towels and cleaned off all the dust and cobwebs. Then they hung it on a newly hammered nail in its old spot above the sofa.

Gregory looked at the swirls of dawn colors that hovered over the restless, sparkling ocean waves that filled the canvas. His mom had painted it when he was a baby. It was for him.

"It's beautiful, Mom."

"I thought for a few awful moments this morning that I had lost you, too," she said. "And then when you walked in that door, I realized how much I have to be thankful for. I've been living so much in the dark since Daddy died, and I believe he would want me to step back into the sunshine. Well," she said, waving a hand at the painting, "this is sunshine to my soul, just like you are Gregory, and it's not going to sit down there in the dark cellar anymore."

"It looks good, hanging where it used to be."

"Yes, it does," she said, folding her arms around him from behind. Together, they studied it.

"I love it," said Gregory with a nod.

"Me, too," said his mom, and he could hear the smile in her voice.

TWENTY

Running Free

Later that afternoon, Gregory was sound asleep on the living room sofa when the phone rang.

"Wake up, sleepy head," said his mom and handed him the phone. "It's Matthew."

"Hey, Matt."

"Hey, Gregory. Are you coming tonight for movie night? Dad downloaded *Winnaker Wrecks the World* for us."

Gregory rubbed his eyes. He felt a little disoriented. "That sounds great. Didn't know it was out yet on DVD. What time is it, anyway?"

There was a pause as Matt consulted his watch. "4:46."

"Oh, boy. I've been asleep most of the day."

"Are you sick?"

"No. Just really tired. Good now, though."

"Well, are you coming to see *Winnaker*?"

"Yes," said Gregory. "It's supposed to be really good."

"Great," said Matt. "I have to run up to the Jiffy Mart and get some bread for supper, and I'll get some microwave popcorn for us, too."

"I'll come with you," said Gregory, sitting up and suddenly smiling.

"What?"

"I said I'll come with you."

"You sure?"

"Yes, I'm sure," but the second he hung up the phone, he wasn't so sure. He had done it once, but did that mean he could do it again?

Matt was waiting for him. He handed Gregory part of a Sesame Snap, but Gregory shook his head. He had to concentrate. He had to force himself to think about this morning's victory.

As they started up Clarke Street, Gregory again looked down at his runners. The knot was still there in his lace. He told himself that that knot and these runners had carried him up there this morning, and they could do it again.

Matt was strangely silent, except for his loud chewing. Gregory could see him stealing glances at him.

"Can't you eat those more quietly?"

"Sorry. I guess we're trying this Jiffy Mart thing again, right? Do you have a new plan?"

"No."

"Well, what are we doing?"

No answer.

"Are you okay, Gregory?"

"Yes. No. I mean, yes. Maybe." Then he stopped and turned to look at Matt. "I went up to the Jiffy Mart early this morning," he said.

"You did? This morning? Why didn't you tell me? You went all the way up to the Jiffy Mart?"

Gregory nodded. "Yes, I went up there and I stood on the spot where my dad died. I really did do it. But now it seems so long ago, like it wasn't really me, or something. If I did it this morning, why am I so scared now?"

"Never mind about that," shouted Matt. "You did it! That's all that matters. This is terrific," and he began to jump around, play-punching Gregory in first one shoulder then the other.

"Quit it," said Gregory. "Quit it," but Matt was laughing and kept jumping out of range when Gregory tried to get him back.

"This is great," said Matt. Punch, punch. Punch, punch.

"Hey," said Gregory, rubbing his shoulder but laughing now, too. He tried to punch back, but his arms weren't as long as Matt's and he couldn't connect.

"It's super. It's so cool," said Matt. Punch, punch, punch. "Amazing. I can't believe it." Punch. Punch. And suddenly, he was running. "Come on, race you!" he yelled.

And before he knew it, Gregory was running up the sidewalk behind Matt, headed for the Jiffy Mart.

When they got back to the townhouse complex, Gregory said, "Let's tell Teisha." So they did. They knocked on her door and told her right there on the front steps.

"You did what? You stood on the spot? That's fantastic, Gregory," she said, and her eyes were dancing. For a second, he thought she was going to hug him, and his heart did a somersault. But she just gave him her megawatt smile, and it was almost as good.

"I'll grab my sweater and let's go back up there right now, so I can see you do it," and before Gregory or Matt could agree or disagree, she dashed inside and came back out wearing a fuzzy, bright orange sweater. Gregory thought she looked like a sweet little pumpkin.

"Where are you going?" called Tamara from behind them. "I want to come, too."

"No," said Teisha. "We're just going to the Jiffy Mart. You don't need to come. Sobo will be lonely if you come with us."

"No, she won't," said Tamara stamping her feet. "I want to tell Gregory my new joke."

"No," said Teisha, and when Tamara started to pretend-cry, their grandma came to investigate. Teisha spoke to her in a different language. Japanese. It was beautiful, fast and strange, the sounds and rhythms rising and falling like a song.

"It's okay," said Gregory, interrupting. "She can come with us."

Before they were even down the steps, Tamara said, "Knock-knock, Gregory."

"Who's there?"

"Ida."

"Ida who?"

"I dunno," and Tamara laughed herself silly.

Four knock-knock jokes later, they were crossing Henderson, headed for the spot. This time, the trip was even easier for Gregory. Not perfect, but easier.

A week later, when Gregory took his old Green Hornet out of the garage, he discovered it was too small for him. He hadn't ridden it in almost a year. He talked his mom into buying a used Silverado he found online. After he'd cleaned and polished it and put on a new chain, it was almost like new.

Gregory jumped on Green Hornet II, adjusted the pedals, and set off on his inaugural ride. He was still a little nervous, thinking about all the possibilities of disaster, but gradually the fearfulness faded, and the familiar, fantastic feeling of flying started coming back.

TWENTY ONE

The Final Decision

Everyone had worked hard on the Save Our School campaign. Gregory, Matt, and Teisha had been out several more times, knocking on doors, asking for signatures, and putting signs on people's lawns. The online petition had generated quite a few signatures. The petition sheets in the public places where Gregory's mom's posters were displayed had done well, too.

Still, there had been no final word about the closure from the School Board. As time went by and there was still no answer, hope was beginning to fade.

Not that it mattered to Gregory anymore. Now he

was going up to and passing by the Jiffy Mart and the spot almost every day.

Near the end of October, there was a cold snap. In the mornings, frost glistened on the rooftops and sparkled on the grass. One week before Halloween, the first snow came. It was just a little flurry that lasted no more than ten minutes and melted the instant it hit the ground but, still, it was exciting.

After an indoor afternoon recess because of the torrential rain that followed the snow, the PA crackled. Mr. Sylvester's voice filled all the classrooms and hallways of the school.

"Teachers and boys and girls, please excuse this interruption. We have received a call from the Chair of the School Board concerning the Save Our School campaign, and they have made their decision. We're going to hold an Assembly at three o'clock in the gymnasium to share this information with you. Mrs. Clarkson and I have been calling parents and sending emails, inviting anyone who is able to join us for this important announcement. We're hoping many of your parents will be here, too. In any case, we have prepared a letter that is to go home with you tonight. Teachers, please make sure these get distributed after the Assembly. Thank you."

Everyone looked at each other, trying to guess what the School Board's decision was.

"He doesn't sound happy," whispered Gregory.

"Do you think he would have told us if it was good news?" said Matt.

"I think so."

"All right, everyone," said Mr. Gladstone. "We'll find out soon enough what's happening. Let's get back to work."

The gym was packed with parents. They lined the walls and stood in rows two deep at the back. Mr. Sylvester was up on the stage at the microphone, and the white-haired School Council man was standing beside him. Neither was smiling.

"Thank you, everyone, parents, grandparents, Council members, and members of the community, for joining us this afternoon on such short notice. We received a call from Mrs. Webster, the Chair of the School Board, this morning. A decision has been made about the school closure question, and the result has not been in our favor."

A loud murmur of disappointment ran through the gym.

Mr. Sylvester held up his hands for quiet. "But it's not all bad news," he said. "The School Board has granted Centennial Public School a reprieve. The other two schools will close as of the end of December as originally planned, but we here at Centennial will remain open until the end of this academic year."

Another murmur from the crowd.

"I also want to tell you how impressed the School Board has been with our Save Our School campaign and all the efforts of our students and teachers, our wonderful School Council, you the parents and the community at large, to keep this school open."

One person started to clap, and suddenly the whole gym was filled with the sound of applause.

"Mrs. Webster told us that the School Board has done everything in its power to find a way to keep this historic school site open but, out of financial necessity, it has proved impossible. She also told us some very good news. None of the teachers is going to lose their job or be made redundant. There will be some placement and assignment changes, but these will be made in discussion with individual teachers and teaching assistants. Mrs. Webster has confirmed to me that the School Board will ensure that everyone is comfortable with the changes."

More applause.

Gregory looked over at Mr. Gladstone. He looked pleased.

"I hope Mr. Gladstone will be at the new school," said Gregory. "Wouldn't it be cool if he was our teacher again next year?"

Matt nodded. "What's the name of the new school, anyway?"

As if in answer to his question, Mr. Sylvester said, "I have arranged a tour of Red Maple Drive Consolidated Public School for all our students next week. Parents are invited to attend, as well. We won't all be going on the same day. We'll go by divisions. I'm told the new school is beautiful."

Mr. Sylvester went on to describe it, but Gregory was thinking about Math Club. Would Mr. Singh be there, and would there even be a Math Club?

The next day, Mr. Gladstone answered their flood of questions and told the class that, yes, he was going to be teaching at Red Maple Drive the following September. Everyone cheered. "But," he said, "I'm going to be teaching Grade 6 again, not Grade 7."

There were loud groans from everyone. "However," he continued, "I am planning to assist Mr. Singh with

Math Club. Red Maple Drive is such a big school, we expect there'll be lots of students interested in joining, so the Club will need two leaders."

"Mr. Singh is going to be there?" said Gregory. "There's going to be a Math Club?"

"Yes and yes," said Mr. Gladstone.

TWENTY TWO

Halloween

Gregory and Matt hurried out of the school. "Nine is the only number," said Gregory, "that, when you square it, produces digits that add up to the original number. See?" he said, and held out a piece of paper for Matt: "9 times 9 equals 81, and 8 plus 1 equals 9. Cool, eh? But that's not all. See ... 99 times 9 equals 891, and 999 times 9 equals 8991 ... see the pattern?"

When they got to the bike stands, Teisha and Tamara hurried to catch up with them. Tamara still had on her princess Halloween costume she'd worn in the Primary Grade Parade at lunch time.

"Meet me at my house at 7:00 PM sharp," said Teisha. "I don't want to be late going out trick-or-treating. Don't forget to wear your costumes!" and she and Tamara headed down the sidewalk.

"Well, duh!" said Matt. "Who died and made her boss?" but Gregory just shrugged.

"That's Teisha," he said.

They hopped on their bikes, passed Teisha and Tamara and all the other walkers, and headed down Henderson. As they passed the Jiffy Mart, Gregory thought how nice it was not to be taking the long way home anymore. How had he done it for so long?

When the road was clear, they crossed the intersection, hurtled down Clarke, and raced in through the crooked pillars.

At 6:58, it was already pitch-black out. The sky was clear and the crisp, sharp smells of autumn were all around. It was a perfect night for Halloween.

Gregory and Matt walked past jack-o'-lanterns, scarecrows, and stalks of corn, decorating people's doorways. When they got to Teisha's, there were already lots of kids out, laughing and yelling and running around. Mrs. Mori, Teisha and Tamara's mom, was taking Tamara trick-or-treating. Gregory, Matt, and Teisha were heading out on their own.

Gregory adjusted his Count Dracula fangs and knocked on Teisha's door. For once, Teisha was late. Gregory and Matt waited for her in the little front hallway. Teisha's grandmother gave them each a bag of chips and let them take however many chocolate treats they wanted from a big basket. When Teisha came down the steps, Gregory stared. She was dressed in a red and gold Japanese kimono. Her hair was piled up on top of her head, and tucked in on one side was a big red flower. She had red lipstick on and long black eyelashes. Gregory felt his heart go "thump."

"Oh, you guys look terrific," laughed Teisha.

"You, too," said Gregory.

"Yah," said Matt, a chip halfway to his mouth. "What did you do?"

"What do you mean?" said Teisha. "I got dressed up for Halloween, same as you. Come on. Let's go."

Their first stop was Miss Marshall's. "Trick or treat!" they yelled, and Miss Marshall opened the door. Sam was there with Mickey. The big dog was smiling and wagging his tail. There were mouse ears on his head.

"See," said Sam, "... Mickey Mouse!" She was too old,

she told them, to go trick-or-treating anymore. But her mom had to work and, rather than stay home alone, she'd decided to go to Miss Marshall's and help her give out treats. Not that there were many kids who ventured down Sprucewood Lane. But some of the older ones did.

Their second stop, before hitting the houses on the other streets, was the Jiffy Mart. The night seemed darker when they left Miss Marshall's. The wind had risen and the giant trees rustled high above their heads. Every now and then, a bright patch of sky opened up between the swaying branches. The moon, sitting like a lopsided egg, glared down at them.

They walked faster. Matt's flashlight barely illuminated the gravelly road ahead. Gregory shivered and wished he'd worn a jacket under his costume. Suddenly, an owl screeched, a loud, unearthly sound.

In the dark, Gregory felt Teisha grab his hand. It lasted only a second, but her hand in his felt so warm, so soft, so wonderful. Better even than a perfectly balanced equation. Better even than 7.5.

Then he remembered 37.0. Teisha's favorite number. It had been rolling around inside his head for weeks and he kept forgetting to ask her what made it so special.

"It's normal human body temperature, silly," she said. "In Celsius degrees, of course."

"In Celsius degrees, of course," mimicked Matt.

But Gregory turned and looked at Teisha and thought he'd never seen a more beautiful girl. He reached out and took her hand. "37.0 is a perfect number," he said. "*The* perfect number." And then the three of them were running and laughing, their loot bags banging against their legs, and Gregory's vampire cape sailing straight out behind. He was thinking about temperature and how it's measured, and speed and weight and time. And then all those other things that are so difficult to measure. Things like happiness.

I wonder what the equation for happiness looks like, thought Gregory. And then he realized, he already knew.

Photo credit: Robert Deutsch

An Interview with Beverley Terrell-Deutsch

Beverley, you have created an interesting cast of characters in *Running Scared*. Do you have a favorite character?

Gregory is my favorite character. He was the first character to "come to life" for me when I started writing this story. In fact, he's the reason I wrote the story. He arrived in my imagination as a complete person, with all his quirkiness, fears, strengths, and challenges. Prior to writing *Running Scared*, I had read a very cool book, *SUPER MATH-E-MAGICS!!!*, by V.A. Stephen Lenaghan. That book sparked the idea for me to have Gregory be a math whiz and also provided some of Gregory's advanced thinking about mathematical concepts. Thanks, Mr. Lenaghan!

Are any of the characters based on anyone you know?

None of the characters in *Running Scared* is based on specific people I know. I think each of my characters is more a combination of personality and physical characteristics of different people I know, of acquaintances or even strangers I have observed, or of people I've read about or seen on tv or in the movies. Mostly, though, as was the case with Gregory, my characters tend to arrive in my mind as complete people.

What was your favorite scene in *Running Scared* to write?

My favorite scene to write was the one where Gregory triumphs over his fears and goes to the Jiffy Mart, incredibly, running part of the way, and stands on the spot where his dad died. That scene flowed like a movie through my imagination and I just wrote down what I saw. It was like magic.

What was the hardest scene to write?

The easiest scene to write was the accident scene because I was involved in a similar car crash. I know what it feels like when the air bags explode, and I have experienced that millisecond of uncertainty when it's over ... "Am I dead? Is this heaven?" However, thankfully, no one was badly hurt in that accident.

The hardest scene for me to write was the one where Gregory and the dog have a stand-off. I needed to convey Gregory's fear as he stared into the face and fangs of the lion-dog, but at the same time leave open the possibility that the dog was actually more scared himself than scary. That was difficult.

What was your favorite subject when you were in grade six?

Language was my favorite subject. I always loved reading, all through school. In Grade 6, the stories became more interesting, more complex, and I loved that. What I didn't like, though, was having to answer in writing what I thought were the boring questions that were part of the "Responding" or "What do you think?" activities at the end of each story. I always hurried through that part, eager to get on to the next story.

Were you afraid of anything when you were Gregory's age?

No, thankfully, nothing in particular. I did have the normal childhood fears of "the dark," (so spooky), and "the dentist" (don't tell my current dentist, who is wonderful and always makes jokes just when I've got my mouth wide open, and then I have trouble laughing). But, worst of all, I worried about having to play baseball as part of the PE program at school. I was afraid of that ball; it always came so fast, and it didn't matter whether I was trying to catch it or hit it, it was always faster than me.

Are you afraid of anything now?

Again, no, thankfully, just all the usual stuff that grown-ups tend to worry about and be afraid of, such as speaking in public (it's getting better), performing in public (playing the handbells or the piano ... I need to practice more), eating too much junk food and not enough fruits and vegetables, or buying a Final Sale item that I thought fit me but, upon arriving home, discovering it doesn't ... that kind of thing.

Have you always liked writing stories?

I have always loved writing. Even when I was little. I remember once, when I was in Grade 4, having a great idea for a story and writing it out fast and furiously in pencil, several long pages. But my hand got tired and I wrote more and more lightly, with less and less pressure on the pencil, eager only to get the ideas out of my brain and onto the paper. However, when I came to read the story later, I couldn't even see it. It was too light. It was as if the story had been written in invisible ink and had disappeared from the page. I tried to read it out loud to the class, but struggled and held it up to the light this way and that way, all to no avail. The teacher finally asked me to sit down. That taught me a valuable lesson: ideas are important, for sure, but never underestimate the importance of technology.

Do you have another job besides writing?

Not now, I don't. I am focused on my writing at the moment. But I was an elementary school teacher (I loved teaching the junior grades) and am a psychologist and have worked with hundreds of children of all ages, and teens, and their families and teachers. Of course, specific information about individuals is totally confidential and would never be revealed, but I am fortunate to be able to bring that rich and varied background of experience to my writing.

Are you working on another book now?

Yes. I'm so glad you asked. I'm working on a second book about Gregory and his friends, a sequel to *Running Scared*. It will probably be titled "Running" something-or-other, such as "Running Wild," or "Running Blind," or "Running Away," but I'm not sure yet. The story will tell me later what it wants to be called.

Can you tell us anything about it?

Gregory finds a mysterious letter when he's going through the boxes of his father's belongings that have been sitting in their basement for over a year. This letter, and the many questions it raises, provide the incentive for Gregory and Matt to take a trip to investigate. Teisha and Tamara have their own complicated difficulties when their father must move away to another city.